Sons of Sigurd

Driven by revenge, redeemed by love

When Sigurd, King of Maerr on Norway's west coast, was assassinated and his lands stolen, his five sons, Alarr, Rurik, Sandulf, Danr and Brandt, were forced to flee for their lives.

The brothers swore to avenge their father's death, and now the time has come to fulfill their oath. They will endure battles, uncover secrets and find unexpected love in their quest to reclaim their lands and restore their family's honor!

Join the brothers on their quest in

Stolen by the Viking by Michelle Willingham
Falling for Her Viking Captive by Harper St. George
Conveniently Wed to the Viking by Michelle Styles
Redeeming Her Viking Warrior by Jenni Fletcher

And the story continues with

Tempted by Her Viking Enemy by Terri Brisbin

Coming soon!

"So what does it feel like?"

Sissa gave him a puzzled look and lay down again, one hand resting beneath her cheek.

"What?" Danr paused with the flagon against his lips.

"Mating? *How* is it pleasurable?"

"Moon's eye, woman." He spun his face toward her again. "I'm trying to be good!"

"But you just said that it was pleasurable!"

"It is. *Very* pleasurable sometimes, but I'm trying to be good with *you*. You're an innocent."

"But *I* asked."

He muttered something under his breath. "All right. It's like losing yourself. You don't think, you just feel."

"Mmm." She rolled onto her back again, feeling even more curious. Could *mating* really be as pleasurable as he said? Would it be pleasurable with him?

It wasn't until he inhaled sharply that she realized she'd just asked the question aloud. Heat flooded her body...

JENNI FLETCHER

—

Redeeming Her
Viking Warrior

Recycling programs
for this product may
not exist in your area.

ISBN-13: 978-1-335-50571-2

Redeeming Her Viking Warrior

Copyright © 2020 by Jenni Fletcher

This edition published by arrangement with Harlequin Books S.A.

For questions and comments about the quality of this book,
please contact us at CustomerService@Harlequin.com.

Harlequin Enterprises ULC
22 Adelaide St. West, 40th Floor
Toronto, Ontario M5H 4E3, Canada
www.Harlequin.com

Printed in U.S.A.

Jenni Fletcher was born in the north of Scotland and now lives in Yorkshire with her husband and two children. She wanted to be a writer as a child but became distracted by reading instead, finally getting past her first paragraph thirty years later. She's had more jobs than she can remember but has finally found one she loves. She can be contacted on Twitter, @jenniauthor, or via her Facebook Author page.

Books by Jenni Fletcher

Harlequin Historical

The Warrior's Bride Prize
Reclaimed by Her Rebel Knight

Sons of Sigurd

Redeeming Her Viking Warrior

Regency Belles of Bath

An Unconventional Countess

Secrets of a Victorian Household

Miss Amelia's Mistletoe Marquess

Whitby Weddings

The Convenient Felstone Marriage
Captain Amberton's Inherited Bride
The Viscount's Veiled Lady

Visit the Author Profile page
at Harlequin.com for more titles.

For the Carnforth Rowlinsons, especially my mum, who has all the strength, stoicism and courage we associate with Viking heroines, with extra hugs.

Also a huge thank you to Rachel for all her advice and cookery books.

Prologue

The woman appeared out of nowhere. One moment Danr Sigurdsson was alone, his body cradled amid the tangled roots of an oak tree, the next she was looming above him, the spear in her hand pointing straight at his throat.

He stared up at her, absently wondering who she was and where she'd come from, then gave up the effort and closed his eyes. His head and chest were throbbing. So, too, was his pulse, so hard and fast it felt as though his heart were trying to force its way through his ribcage.

Considering how much blood he'd lost over the past few hours he was surprised it could still summon the strength to beat at all, but at least the pain in his arm was fading to numbness now. If he kept still, he could almost forget the angry, red gouge where the blade had caught him, slicing through skin and muscle and tendon. If he didn't move at all, scarcely allowing himself to breathe, in fact, he could forget almost everything.

The rustle of leaves overhead had already faded to a dull murmur and the light behind his eyelids was dimming, narrowing around the edges like a tunnel collapsing in on itself, enveloping him in darkness.

Something prodded his neck and he prised his eyelids open again. It was the woman, the blunt edge of her spear nudging lightly against his skin. What did she want? Was she threatening him? If she was, then she didn't need to. At that moment he couldn't have put up a fight with a kitten.

The very air felt heavy, pinning him to the ground as if there were a fallen tree lying across his chest. He was going to die whether she impaled him or not and he wasn't going to protest either way. Perhaps it was best that she went ahead and put him out of his misery quickly. He would have failed his brothers— *again*—but at least it would have been while trying to fulfil his oath.

He curled the fingers of his good arm around the hilt of his sword, Bitterblade, determined to die like a warrior even if he couldn't fight back, but the woman didn't move as much as a muscle. As far as he could tell, she didn't even blink. He felt a flicker of unease, wondering if she were some figment of his imagination or apparition. She looked like one, her narrow, expressionless face streaked with grey smudges while her hair tumbled in such wild, half-braided, half-loose disarray that it resembled a cloak of golden hay around her shoulders. She was a lot like a spear herself, he thought, sleek and slender with a flat chest and shoulders the same width as her hips, though he hated himself for noticing. Apparently it was true what Rurik had always said: Danr would still be looking at women on his deathbed… Well, here he was on it now, though perhaps it was only fitting. A woman had brought him into the world, albeit reluctantly, and now a woman was going to take him out of it. It would be a fitting revenge for all the ones he'd known and discarded in between.

He waited, feeling increasingly uneasy beneath her silent scrutiny. Even from where he lay on the ground he could see that her eyes were pale and striking, like oyster pearls, mirroring the sky behind her head, an iridescent grey speckled with flakes of silver that looked a lot like…*snow?*

Somehow he dragged a laugh up out of his chest. This was truly the end, then. He hadn't even realised that it was cold enough—or late enough in the year—for snow, though now he thought about it he could see whispery coils of air emerging from his mouth. From hers, too, which at least proved she was a real flesh-and-blood woman, no matter how spectral she seemed. Snow was filling the air all around them, covering his broken and bloodied body in a gauzy white layer. After everything that he and his brothers had gone through, after they'd travelled so far and fought so many enemies from Maerr to Eireann to Constantinople to Alba, now he was going to die here in a forest all on his own and be buried in snow. His body would probably lie where it was for months, encased in ice, refusing to rot away until spring. Maybe Hilda would be the one to eventually find him and know that she'd won.

He gave a grunt of disgust and then froze, the hairs on the back of his neck rising at the sound of an answering growl. With an effort he lifted his head, his already pounding heartbeat redoubling in speed at the sight of a wolf—no, *two* wolves—stalking through the undergrowth towards him, their teeth bared in twin snarls, no doubt drawn by the scent of his blood.

Quickly, he shifted his gaze back to the woman, trying to convey a warning with his eyes since his throat was too dry to speak, but she appeared not to notice, her expression unreadable as the wolves came to stand on either side of her like a pair of dark sentinels. Maybe she really was an apparition after all, Danr thought with a shudder, an unforgiving ice maiden like the ones of which his mother had told him and Rurik as boys, a supernatural force able to control the animals of the forest as well as the elements. If she were, then he was entirely at her mercy. She could do whatever she wanted and there was nothing he could do to stop her.

He swallowed, waiting for her to decide his fate. At least a spear would be quick, whereas being torn apart by wolves… Surely not even *he* deserved that?

Did he?

He dropped his head back to the ground and closed his eyes for a few seconds, feeling the kiss of cold flakes on his lids and lashes, but when he opened them again she was gone and the wolves were nowhere to be seen. All he could see was snow.

Chapter One

Six hours earlier

It *couldn't* be this easy.

Danr stood among the trees at the edge of the forest, watching a solitary figure walking along the stony shore of the sea loch below. He could see only the side of her face, but there was no doubt in his mind that it was Hilda. Even if it hadn't been for the braid of dark hair hanging down to her knees, there was the familiar stiff posture, the self-important tilt of her head and the imperiously raised chin. He didn't need to see her expression to know what it would be. She'd wielded it against him for twenty-two years, the arrogant look that proclaimed *she* was the only woman in Maerr who mattered—who'd *ever* mattered; she was Jarl Sigurd's wife, a hundred times more important than Danr's dead mother who had been his concubine.

Not any more.

Three years ago, everything had changed. The

bloody massacre on his half-brother Alarr's wedding day had brought the world they'd known crashing down around their ears, destroying their home, their security and their family's reputation all in one fell swoop. Their father, the mighty Sigurd, had been murdered alongside Alarr's betrothed, Gilla, his elder half-brother Brandt's wife, Ingrid, and several of the helmsmen who'd tried to defend them. No one in Maerr had been the same since, especially Danr and Rurik and their half-brothers Brandt, Alarr and Sandulf. Afterwards, their need for answers and vengeance had eclipsed all other concerns, including holding on to their father's kingdom. Eventually they'd all left their homeland in pursuit of the assassins while the widowed Hilda had fled to the island of Skíð on the west coast of Alba with their father's former helmsman, Joarr.

At first, her hasty remarriage less than a year after her husband's murder had seemed a reasonable response to all the political upheaval in Maerr, but now there were questions, significant ones, that needed answers. Which was why he was there on Skíð, *just* for answers. That was the agreement he'd made with Sandulf when they'd parted ways. He was there to confront Hilda with the evidence they'd uncovered and demand an explanation. Under no circumstances was he to seek retribution, no matter *what* that explanation turned out to be. Of course, Sandulf was still looking for alternative answers, not wanting to believe his mother guilty of any involvement in the massacre, but Danr's intuition told him the opposite. Between them, the five sons of Sigurd were closing in on whoever had sent the assassins and he *knew* Hilda was involved somehow. All he needed to do was prove it.

But it couldn't be this easy. He'd been on the island for less than a day and there she was, the very first person he came across, alone and seemingly unarmed. It was much too easy. He was known for his cunning, for his well-laid plans and clever stratagems in battle, for never rushing in without looking at a situation from all angles first, but at that moment he didn't care. His temper flared like a torch dipped in oil at the sight of her. He wanted answers and he was going to get them any way he could. *Now.*

He threw one last cautious look up and down the beach, making sure that no one else was in sight before striding purposefully across the pebbles towards her. The sea loch was long and narrow, bordered by rolling hills and thick forest on the south-western edge of the island, with impressive views of the mountains that rose up like stone giants to the north. At any other time he might have stopped to admire the jagged ridges and snow-capped pinnacles in the distance, but now his vision seemed to be glazed with red.

Hilda turned at the last moment, alerted by the sound of crunching stones beneath his feet, her welcoming smile turning immediately to a look of surprise and hostility. *That* was familiar, too. Obviously her low opinion of him hadn't mellowed in the three years since they'd left Maerr and the feeling was more than mutual.

'*You?*' She kept her haughty chin raised.

'Me.' Danr curled his lip in a pretence of a smile. 'It's been a long time, Stepmother. Did you miss me?'

If he hadn't been so angry, he might have laughed at the way her whole body stiffened, like wood petrifying before his very eyes. She'd always hated him calling her that—which was exactly the reason he did it so often. His very existence—and that of his twin brother, Rurik—was a source of deep-seated resentment for her, a resentment that had only grown stronger since their mother's death when Sigurd had brought them to live in his own hall. For as long as Danr could remember, Hilda had done her best to ignore the two boys, as if by doing so she could wilfully forget her husband's infidelity, too. His quieter twin had responded in kind, but Danr had chosen the opposite approach of baiting her at every opportunity he got. And he saw absolutely no reason to stop now.

'What are you doing here?' Hilda's voice positively seethed with dislike.

'Can't I come for a visit?' He spread his arms out as if he expected her to embrace him, knowing full well she would have preferred to walk over hot coals. For his part, he would rather have hugged a snake. 'For old times' sake?'

'No!'

'That's not very hospitable.'

'I'm not feeling very hospitable.' She looked past him, her expression turning hopeful. 'Is Brandt with you? Alarr? Sandulf?'

'No.' He took pleasure in her obvious disappointment. 'I came alone.'

'Why? What do you want, Danr?'

'Straight to the point, as always.' He laid a hand on the pommel of his sword, drumming his fingers lightly against it. 'I want the same thing my brothers want: the truth about who killed our father.'

'We all want that!' She sounded impatient. 'It still doesn't explain what you're doing here.'

'Doesn't it?' He let his fingers go still, lowering his voice to an undertone and allowing his smile to fade slowly. 'Can you think of no reason at all?'

'What?' The air between them seemed to thicken with tension as her eyes widened and then darted towards the village at the far end of the beach. 'Maybe we should talk inside.'

'I thought you just said I wasn't welcome?' He lifted an eyebrow mockingly.

'You're not, but it's getting colder. The wind's changed direction.'

'Then we'd better make this quick. Tell me why you murdered my father and I'll be on my way.' He said the words casually, as if they were of no importance, but it felt good to accuse her, to see her jaw plummet and hear her sharp intake of breath.

'I didn't murder Sigurd!'

'Maybe not by your own hand, but *someone* ordered the attack.'

'Not me! Why would I do such a thing?'

'Because you didn't love him.'

'No.' She didn't even pause to deny it. 'Not for a long time, but that doesn't mean I wanted him dead.'

'You didn't want him as your husband any more.'

Danr advanced a step closer, deliberately trying to intimidate her. 'You didn't want him in your bed.'

'He didn't want to be in it either!' Hilda's green eyes glittered with contempt. 'That proves nothing. How many of the women you sleep with do *you* love, Danr? Any at all? But you don't kill them to be rid of them.'

'That's different.' He felt a fresh burst of temper. 'You were betraying my father with his own helmsman and he found out about it. Brandt heard them arguing a few days before the attack.'

'Sigurd only suspected.' Hilda snorted dismissively. 'He didn't know.'

'Then it makes even more sense that you killed him. You ordered the attack before he could find proof and punish your lover.'

'No!'

'*That's* why you ran away with Joarr so soon afterwards.'

'It wasn't soon!' She tossed her braid at the accusation. 'I stayed in Maerr for months to nurse Alarr and help Brandt hold on to his birthright, but they were both so set upon revenge. Everything was falling apart and my sister…' She bit her tongue, seeming to think better of whatever it was she'd been about to say. 'Joarr said it was too dangerous for us to remain. That's why we came to find shelter here with his kinsmen.'

'You mean, in case someone discovered what you'd done?'

'*Enough!*' She thrust her jaw out angrily. 'How dare you say such things! When my sons discover what you're accusing me of—'

'Ah, but who do you think sent me?' Danr gave a slow, taunting smile. 'Only, they're good sons. They don't want to accuse their own mother, especially when they have a bastard brother who's more than willing to do it for them. I left Sandulf only a matter of days ago.'

He paused to let the words sink in, pleased to see her face blanch. Unfortunately, he was no closer to getting a confession. Perhaps accusing her outright hadn't been the best tactic after all. Perhaps he ought to have bided his time and confronted her with the evidence first, or, better still, spoken to Joarr beforehand as he'd planned, but his temper had got the better of him. If he couldn't provoke her into an admission of guilt, then he only had one other option left. It was a bluff, though doubtless she despised him enough to believe him capable of it…

'Admit you had a hand in it…' he drew Bitterblade in one slick, steady motion '…and I'll let your sons decide on your punishment. Otherwise this is between you and me.'

'I admit nothing.' She didn't even flinch, the look in her eyes only hardening. 'I just told you I wasn't involved.'

'I don't believe you.'

'Then kill me if you must, but I refuse to stand here and be judged by a man like *you*. You may be able to charm the birds from the trees, Danr, but you'll always be worthless underneath. You take a different woman into your bed every night because you think it makes you more of a man, but it makes you less. You inherited the very worst traits of your father. You're empty inside, Danr. You have no depth, no heart, no honour or decency.'

'Say what you want about me, but you will not insult my father!' Danr took a step closer, pointing the tip of his sword at her breast.

'Why not? He insulted me every day of our marriage. He insulted me with your mother—with you!'

'Maybe you deserved it!'

'Get away from her!'

Danr spun around at the sound of Joarr's shout, furious at himself for having been caught off guard. He had to give credit to Hilda. She hadn't betrayed her new husband's approach by as much as a twitch of an eyelid. She'd known just how to distract him, too, stoking his temper at the same time as he'd been trying to provoke hers. Now the giant warrior was only a few feet away and advancing steadily, sword and shield both raised, his expression angrier than Danr had ever seen it, redolent with bloodlust, and no wonder. From a distance it must have looked as if he'd been about to cut Hilda down in cold blood.

'Did he touch you?' Joarr's gaze slid briefly towards his wife.

'No.' To Danr's surprise, there was actually a placatory note in Hilda's voice. 'He's come from Sandulf. It seems that my sons have some suspicions about me.'

'What kind of suspicions?'

'About Sigurd's death. They think I was involved.'

'You?' Joarr's stopped a sword's length away from Danr, his eyes like chips of blue ice. 'She had no part in it. *That's* your answer.'

'Is that what she told you?'

'It's what I know.'

'Something tells me you're not the best judge of character where she's concerned.'

'I believe my wife.'

Danr blew air between his teeth contemptuously. 'And you always said I was the one who was driven by lust. Apparently you're guilty of the same weakness, old friend.'

'I love Hilda and she loves me.' Joarr drew his brows together in a ferocious line. 'Is love so hard for you to understand, boy?'

'Yes!' Danr answered without thinking, though it was only the truth. He loved his brothers, but love for a woman, the kind that Alarr had found with Breanne, Rurik with Annis, and Sandulf with Ceanna, *that* had never made sense to him. It never would. His mother's love for his father had brought her only pain and regret. Just the thought of it filled him with anger.

'She needs to pay for what she did.' He jerked his head towards Hilda, his ragged temper fraying even further.

'She didn't *do* anything!'

'Then ask her why the assassins had some of her jewellery—three pendants.'

'Pendants?' Hilda's voice seemed to crack on the word.

'Aye. The ones you used to pay them.'

'What kind of—?'

'She'll explain nothing!' Joarr's roar was like a crack

of thunder. 'You always talked too much, Danr. You should have been a skald, not a warrior.'

'Wait!' Hilda lifted her hands as if she were trying to calm them both. 'Perhaps we *should* talk.'

'It's too late for that.' Joarr waved his shield in her direction, gesturing for her to get back. 'He just threatened you. That's reason enough for me to kill him.'

'You can try!'

Danr gave a harsh laugh, shifting his weight to his right foot as he waited for the older man to attack first. It didn't take long. Barely a second after he'd issued the challenge, Joarr rammed the boss of his shield forward, attempting to knock him down, but Danr was faster, moving to the left, parrying the thrust aimed after him and then darting forward, running his blade across the warrior's mail coat as he went.

The old helmsman gave a grunt of anger and whirled around, slicing his shield through the air with such bloodthirsty force that Danr had to duck to a crouching position to avoid having his skull smashed. He used the position to strike at Joarr's legs, aiming a kick at his kneecaps to send him reeling backwards, but the helmsman recovered quicker than Danr had expected, charging forward again almost immediately and knocking him sideways. It was a foolish attack, one that left Joarr's right flank exposed and unprotected. If Danr lifted his blade then, it would be easy enough to skewer him in the armpit. There was a gap in his mail. He could see it—a clear, almost perfect target. If he chose, he could sink his blade there and then cut Hilda down where she stood. He could finish them both in a matter of moments. The killing blow was his for the taking. *If...*

He hesitated as a succession of memories swept through his mind: Joarr teaching him how to hold his first wooden sword, how to wield it, how to use his opponents' weaknesses against them, giving him ten times more attention than his real father ever had... How could he use those lessons against him now? How could he kill him? He *couldn't*, he realised, jumping aside just in time to dodge another blow that sent a flurry of pebbles up into the air where he'd just stood. All he wanted was to knock him down long enough to talk, to explain to him how he knew Hilda was guilty...

He circled around, knowing that, if he started to give ground, the pummelling would be relentless. Joarr was a hulk of a man and a fearsome fighter, though his size and age made him slow. Fortunately for Danr, after years of training together, he knew all of the man's tactics, whereas his own range of manoeuvres had expanded and been honed by necessity over the past couple of years. If it hadn't been for the rib he'd injured in Alba, then he might have found a way to end the fight already, but he still wanted to do so without hurting his former teacher. This wasn't the fight he wanted. If they could only put down their weapons and talk man to man as the friends they'd once been...

There was a sound of shouting and Danr turned his head sharply, grimacing at the sight of at least a dozen warriors emerging from the village at the end of the beach, all running to Hilda and Joarr's rescue. He gritted his teeth and muttered a string of the most

colourful oaths he could think of. He'd wasted his opportunity with Hilda and run out of time. All he could
do now was escape to the forest while he still had the
chance, then take some time to consider and come up
with a better plan. That was what he *ought* to do, but
when he tried to move something felt wrong.

He glanced down in bewilderment. His right arm
felt strangely numb and his fingers seemed to be having trouble keeping a grip on his sword... The moment
he thought it, the blade fell from his grasp, hitting the
ground with a heavy clatter. That was when he noticed
the gash in his mail, accompanied by a searing burst of
pain. The metal links must have torn when Joarr had
charged him, allowing his sword to find its target for a
moment. He had no memory of the blade even touching him, though obviously it had.

He touched his fingers to the hot stream of blood
trickling down his arm and then looked back at Hilda.
Confusingly, her hands were wrapped around Joarr's
waist as if she were holding him back, restraining him
even, while the warriors from the village were coming
ever closer. If he stayed where he was then he'd be captured and executed for certain, which in itself wouldn't
matter so much, but it wouldn't give his brothers the
answers they needed either. That was why he was there
and why he had to survive. For them.

He picked up Bitterblade with his good arm, took a
few steps back towards the forest, then ran.

Chapter Two

Sissa gathered the few items she needed into a pack, flung two of the warmest furs she could find over her shoulders, then made her way back through the trees to where she'd found the injured man. The snow had already stopped, but she didn't hold out much hope of finding him still alive. If the amount of blood on the ground around his body was any indication, he'd be a corpse by the time she returned, but if he wasn't…well then, she'd do what she could to save him, whether he wanted her to or not. There had been a curious expression on his face when she'd nudged her spear against his throat—just a gentle push to see if he was still alive—almost ambivalence, as if he were ready to die. But she was a healer, not a killer, and she'd seen more than enough death already.

He was sprawled exactly where she'd left him, his head propped against the roots of an oak tree. From a distance, he certainly looked dead, but as she leaned over she could just make out the slight flutter of a pulse

in his jaw. She laid her pack aside and pressed two
fingers against his jaw. Weak, but still beating. The
neck beneath was lean and muscular, like all the rest
of him, she noticed. There didn't seem to be a hint of
fat anywhere on his body, especially his face where his
prominent cheekbones stood out like sharp blades. She
slid her hand upwards and pressed her palm against his
cheek. The skin was cold—unsurprisingly, when he
was half-buried in a layer of snow—but his skin had a
waxy pallor, too. Between his injury and the weather
it was impossible to guess which would kill him first.
She'd have to remove his damp clothes somehow, but
for now...

Frowning, she pulled one of the furs from her shoulder and draped it over his legs and chest before turning her attention to the wound itself. By the look of
it he'd torn a strip from the hem of his under-tunic
and tied it around the top of his arm to try to stop the
flow of blood, but by now the fabric was saturated and
useless. She unravelled it carefully and looked closer.
There were no signs of infection, which meant that the
wound was still fresh—a few hours old at most—and
obviously made with a blade. Only a sword or dagger
could have sliced so cleanly, though fortunately the
gash wasn't as bad as she'd first feared, being long
rather than deep.

The man writhed weakly as she poured water from
a flask to wash away the dirt, then rubbed a combination of wild garlic and powdered oak bark over the sur-
face to staunch the bleeding. Next she applied a layer
of dried sphagnum moss to act as a poultice, before

binding it in place with a piece of cloth. His breathing seemed to become shallower and more laboured as she worked, but she kept her fingers moving, concentrating on the task as if it were the only thing in the world that mattered. Finally, she sat back on her haunches to survey her handiwork. Not bad. He'd survived her ministrations, which was a good sign, but he needed warmth, food and shelter in that order if he was going to survive the night.

She chewed her lip and glanced up at the sky. It was getting dark, the temperature was plummeting and he was far too big for her to drag anywhere. Building a fire, however, seemed like an additional danger. If people were out searching for him—which, given the nature of his injury, seemed likely—then a fire would only draw their attention, but if she *didn't* light one then the cold would likely finish him off first. At that moment it struck her as the lesser of two evils.

She reached into her pack for the dry logs she'd brought just in case and built a small fire an arm's length from where he lay. On the damp ground it took longer than usual, but eventually the flint struck a light. Then, when the flames were hot enough, she removed the fur from his body and considered the rest of him. Most of his clothing consisted of leather and mail which looked reasonably impervious to the elements, but the metal links also looked heavy enough to constrict his breathing and the linen collar around his neck was sodden. Fortunately, his mail was fastened at the front, allowing her to carefully undo the belt buckle and clasps and peel it away to the sides. Next she reached for a knife and carefully cut away his long-sleeved under-tunic, leaving his chest bare, all except for a leather pouch hanging from a cord around his neck.

The sight of his naked torso seemed to steal her breath away for a few seconds, making it falter and then emerge again in quick, slightly shaky bursts. As a healer she'd seen plenty of bodies, but this one was different. It was magnificent, sculpted, as if it were hewn from actual rock. His natural build must be lean, she guessed, running her tongue along the seam of her suddenly dry lips, but there were so many muscles it was impossible to be sure. There were muscles in places she'd never even conceived that muscles could be before. The gash on his arm wasn't the only evidence of recent battles either. There were several long scars across his ribs and a vicious purple bruise on his stomach. She wondered what his last fight had been about and how his opponent had fared. She doubted the combat would have been one-sided. Judging by his well-developed biceps, not to mention the collection of bronze and silver arm rings around them, this man was no stranger to a sword.

The idea made her uncomfortable. He was obviously a warrior, one of that breed of men who thought they could fight their way through life, taking what they wanted by force from those who only wanted to live in peace. Of all men, warriors were the ones she disliked and distrusted the most. So much so that she was almost tempted to get up and leave him to take his chances alone, but she couldn't. At that moment he was injured and helpless and she was the only one who could save him.

She drew the fur back over his chest and studied his face. The lines of pain and tension that had been around his mouth and forehead seemed to have smoothed out since she'd been tending him, making him look younger and quite forbiddingly handsome—hardly like a warrior at all. She hadn't seen him among the new settlers before, she was certain—she would have remembered such a striking face, not to mention his mane of thick golden hair—which meant that he must be new to the island. He reminded her of Birger, a boy from her village years ago. He'd been older than she was, seventeen summers to her thirteen, and so good looking that all the girls had flirted and competed for his attention. She'd watched him, too, hoping that some day he might notice her, though he never had, not really. And then he'd lost the ability to notice anything at all, like everyone else in her village. Everyone except for her and Tove, the only survivors.

She reached a hand out to the wolf who trotted forward at once to lick and then rub her nose against it. Her father had found Tove as an emaciated cub and brought her back to the village to nurse and raise as a guard dog. Sissa had done most of the training and in return the animal had become her constant companion and shadow. She wasn't sure whether Tove saw her as a sister or a mother, but whatever it was they were family. The bond between them had saved her life countless times, beginning with the raid.

A familiar cold sweat broke out on her skin at the

memory and she pushed it aside, reaching for a water skin instead. Carefully, she added some herbs and then poured the liquid down the man's throat, holding his mouth shut as he spluttered. *There*. She rocked back on her heels, satisfied. That was as much as she could do in the dwindling daylight. In the morning, if he was still alive, she'd build a shelter around him, but for now, it was enough.

She wrapped herself up in the other fur and lay down beside the fire, Tove beside her, Halvar stretched out opposite, aloof but always alert. He was part of her family, too, though she suspected he only tolerated her for his mate's sake. They'd all wait together and see what the morning would bring.

Behind her, the warrior mumbled in his sleep. The words were barely distinguishable, a scattering of names and epithets, but he sounded anguished—tormented, even. From the sound of it he was thrashing about, too. Was he dreaming of his last battle? Whatever it was, the tone of his voice sent a shiver down her spine.

She rolled over to make sure he hadn't thrown his fur aside and jumped with surprise to find his eyes wide open, boring into hers with a look of such deep-rooted pain and sorrow that she felt her heart clench before they suddenly closed again.

Another shiver, even colder than before, trickled down her spine like melting ice. For one horrible moment she'd felt as though she'd been looking into a mirror.

She exhaled slowly, buried her face into Tove's fur and wondered if she'd done the right thing by saving his life.

Chapter Three

W<small>AS</small> he dead?

Danr dragged his eyelids open, recognising the bumpy feel of the roots behind his head though not the view above. Instead of the grey sky and falling snow he remembered, there was a screen of branches, all packed together with twigs and moss and intertwined to form a kind of arch.

Was he dead? If he was, then he'd failed his brothers. That thought was horrifying enough, but the fact that he could remember everything was even worse—everything he'd done and felt over the past three years. Guilt, failure, self-loathing…all his familiar companions were still there, as devastating and lucid as ever. He tried sitting up to escape them and then fell back again, the world spinning sickeningly around him as his body was racked with shudders. No Valhalla for him, then. Not that he'd expected to deserve that either.

He heard a soft footfall approaching and tilted his head just in time to see the pale-eyed, spectral-looking woman from his dream slip under the archway. Although, it was less of an archway than a tunnel, he realised now, a makeshift shelter shielding his body from the elements and a skilfully made one, too... Had *she* done it? He clamped his brows together, trying to make sense of the scene. Maybe he wasn't dead, after all. Or dreaming either. Though for a real woman she had a distinctly uncanny aspect, with a mass of untamed, white-gold hair half-obscuring her face as she crouched beside him. Was she Norse or Gael? She had a spiral-shaped torc around her neck, moulded from bronze and open at the throat, though there were no engravings to provide any clue about who she was...

'Did you build this?' He croaked the words out, relieved to find that he could finally speak again.

The woman didn't even glance at his face, let alone answer. Instead, she simply bent over him, unravelling some kind of linen bandage and removing a piece of what looked like moss from his arm before leaning closer. He tensed, very aware of the warm tingle of her breath on his skin as she examined his wound for a few seconds and then covered it over again.

'Is it still snowing out there?' He tried a different question.

Nothing.

'Who are you?' He switched from Norse to Gaelic, but not as much as a flicker of recognition or interest crossed her features.

Danr lifted an eyebrow in surprise. Even if she couldn't understand him, she was obviously aware of his lips moving, but she seemed simply not to care. It was bizarre. Considering the effort she'd apparently put into saving his life, such unresponsive behaviour was…odd.

'Danr.' He raised his good arm to his chest and said his name. 'I'm Da—'

He broke off at the sight of one of the wolves at her back. It had followed her into the tunnel and now looked as if it were considering him as a possible meal. Instinctively, he reached for Bitterblade, but, as he watched, the woman turned and put her hand on the animal's head, making a low humming sound in the back of her throat before leading it outside again.

He exhaled with relief, though his nerves had barely had a chance to recover before she was back again, a cup of some strange-smelling liquid in her hand. He recognised the aroma though he wasn't conscious of having smelled it before, as if it had somehow been a part of his dreams. If 'dreams' was an appropriate word for what he'd gone through. Nightmares combined with horror-filled memories seemed a more appropriate description, all of them revolving around the same day three years ago.

The woman held the cup to his lips and he drank, glad of the distraction. The taste was bearable rather than pleasant, but it soothed his throat and made him feel more relaxed.

'Thank you.' He tried to catch her gaze as she pulled the cup away again, still hoping for some kind of response, but she refused to oblige. It unnerved him, being unable to communicate with her, not having any idea what she was thinking either. He wasn't accustomed to being ignored, especially by women. Most of them were usually more than eager to talk to him, but this one…she was a mystery, tending to his needs without as much as a look or murmur.

Who was she? It was the last thought in his mind before he drifted back to sleep.

What was happening to him now?

Danr stared up at the branches again, wondering what the noise was. This time he was reasonably certain he wasn't dead, though he had the vague impression of having drifted in and out of consciousness over the past few hours…or perhaps days? He had no idea how long he'd been lying in the shelter, but at least he felt better, more like himself again, all except for the loud drumming sound in his ears.

He rolled on to his good side, trying to escape it, only to find the woman lying beside him, curled up beneath a fur with the back of her head only a few inches from his face. He stiffened with shock. Surely they hadn't…? No. Both his mind and body rebelled at the idea. In his current state, he wouldn't have been able to and, even if he had, he'd sworn a solemn oath after the massacre in Maerr. No woman would share his bed, not like *that* anyway, until he'd made amends to his brothers and earned their forgiveness, Brandt and Alarr especially. After he'd achieved that, well, maybe then he'd consider a bedmate again, but he'd never go back to the way he'd been before. He'd never treat sex as a mere sport again. He hadn't even looked at a woman during the past three years, although he had to admit that the sight of the one lying beside him now was unexpectedly stirring.

What was she doing there?

He craned his neck to peer outside. Presumably it was morning, though it was hard to tell just by looking outside the tunnel. The world was a veil of slate grey, interspersed with the darker grey outlines of the forest. The snow seemed to have been replaced by a steady flow of rain, running in fast-flowing rivulets over the ground and pummelling the roof of the shelter like hailstones, which at least explained the drumming sound. He could see the doused remains of a small fire outside, too. That explained the woman's presence. She must have taken shelter beside him, sharing the warmth of the fur and his body to survive. It was the sensible thing to do, although part of him wished that she hadn't, a part that was growing larger and harder by the second. Not that that had anything to do with *her*, he told himself, willing the feeling to subside. She was far too flat-chested and wraith-like for his own personal tastes, not to mention uncommunicative. It was probably just her scent affecting him, slightly musky but with a hint of sweetness, making him want to move closer, to press his lips against the soft-looking curve of her neck and to nuzzle the delicate skin behind her ear...

What would she taste like?

Stars! He swallowed a groan. Three years without a woman were clearly taking their toll.

He tore his gaze away, forcing himself to remember the last time he'd lain with a woman. He hadn't known her name and her face was little more than a blur in his memory, which was particularly ironic considering how attractive he'd found her at the time. Their coupling had been fierce and energetic, and so loud that he'd only become aware of shouts and screams in the distance afterwards. Too late he'd wrenched his clothes back on and charged outside, but the assassins had already done their worst. His home had looked like something out of a nightmare, a burning, wrecked shell of a village... The woman herself had seemed unsurprised by the scene, though by the time the thought had occurred to him, she'd been long gone and no one else had remembered even seeing her. It had been as though she'd simply walked into Maerr with the sole intention of seducing him, which in all likelihood she had, arriving and leaving with the assassins and playing her part to perfection. Not that he'd made it a challenge. A pair of swaying hips and a few provocative looks and he'd followed her out to a barn on the edge of the village like a hound with its tongue hanging out.

You inherited all the very worst traits of your father...

Hilda's scornful words floated back into his mind. She'd never made any secret of her contempt for his womanising and now he had to admit she'd been right to judge him. He *had* been less of a man than his brothers. If his behaviour hadn't been so notorious, then the assassins wouldn't have been able to trick him so easily. If he hadn't allowed himself to be lured away, then he would have been at the wedding and his father, Ingrid and Gilla might still be alive. At the very least he would have died trying to defend them. Instead he had to live with the shame of having survived.

His companion coughed in her sleep and rolled over, stretching her arms above her head like a cat before opening her eyes and looking straight at him. He looked back, experiencing a flash of recognition as if their eyes had met once before—although for the life of him he couldn't remember when—while her own looked surprised and then...nothing, as if she'd just deliberately wiped her expression clean.

But he'd *seen* her surprise. For the briefest of moments her lips had parted, too, as if she'd been about to say something. Which meant that she *could* speak, just like she *could* understand him. He was suddenly certain of it.

He opened his own mouth and then closed it again. All the usual things he might have said to a woman he'd just woken up beside didn't seem quite appropriate somehow. The whole situation felt familiar and yet brand new at the same time. So he waited, gazing into her face while her pale, silvery-grey eyes stared back. It was a curiously intimate feeling, lying side by side with somebody, their breaths intermingling with only the sound of the rain between them, as if time itself were slowing down. He wasn't sure he'd ever looked, *really* looked, at a woman's face before, but now he found himself examining every individual feature as if they might each reveal something new about her. Her forehead was narrow, her chin slightly pointed and her eyes small, with sharply arched brows a shade darker than the rest of her hair, which was the same colour as a wheat field gilded with sunshine. There were still patches of grey on her cheeks, too, and he had to resist the temptation to reach a hand out and wipe them clean. Beneath the smudges and wild tangle of hair, she was…not pretty, exactly, but interesting. Unique. Distinctive. He let his eyes drift lower. Her lips were the most distinctive of all—larger than the rest of her features, with the top one almost as full as the bottom. Somehow just looking at them made his own turn dry.

He didn't know how many moments passed before she sat up abruptly, crawling her way towards the end of the tunnel and curling her legs up beneath her to look out. The rain was so heavy now that it seemed more like small pellets than drips falling out of the sky.

'A good day for sleeping.' Danr heaved himself upright. To his surprise, he managed the feat quite easily. In truth, he felt ten times better now than he had even when he'd woken up, as if just looking at her had somehow helped him. With the obvious exception of his injured arm and some stiffness, his body felt almost completely restored. Whatever she'd done for him, it had obviously worked. He shuffled forward, coming to sit beside her when she didn't answer.

'I hate rain like this. It makes you feel cold and damp just by looking at it, then the clouds hang in the air for days.' He peered out at the grey sky between the trees. 'Although I'm glad to be alive to see it.'

Nothing.

'How long was I asleep?'

Nothing.

'You're a healer.' This time it wasn't a question. 'I'm indebted to you for saving me.'

He stole a sidelong glance at her face when there was still no response. Now that they were no longer lying side by side, he found that he missed looking at her. 'I'd like to repay you.'

Nothing.

'Although it would help if I knew your name?' He lifted an eyebrow hopefully.

Nothing.

'I suppose I could just pick one.' He used the idea as an excuse to lean further forward, trying to catch her eye again. 'Yrsa? Lofn? Gunilla? Astrid? No, I knew an Astrid once. Definitely not Astrid. Marta? Lofn? Ingri—?' He bit his tongue. 'No, not Ingrid. That was the name of my brother's wife, but she…' He shook his head, unable to finish the sentence, but when he looked back, he found her face had turned slightly towards him. Not by much, just enough to suggest she was paying more attention than her continued silence implied. 'What about Bersa?' he carried on, trying not to show that he'd noticed. 'I've never met a Bersa before.'

He'd given up expecting any response so he was taken aback when she twisted her body sideways abruptly, leaning across him to remove the bandage and study his injury again. He froze at the contact. Her face was pressed so close that he could feel the tangled mass of her hair skimming gently against his bicep. It barely counted as a touch, but the feeling made all his muscles clench simultaneously.

'Bersa it is, then.' He cleared his throat, trying to

focus on something else. 'I suppose you're wondering how I ended up like this. It was a mistake. I acted foolishly. I rushed into an argument when I shouldn't have and—'

He sucked in a breath as her fingers brushed against the undamaged skin beneath his wound, infinitely softly but enough to send a torrent of heat coursing through his veins. No, not coursing—*roaring*, as heavy as a waterfall after a flood. It was so unexpected that for a moment he could hardly think straight. Three years had *definitely* been too long if the mere touch of a woman could arouse him so easily, especially the touch of this silent and strange-looking wraith.

She was on her feet so quickly that he was half-afraid he'd said the words out loud. One moment she was retying the bandage around his arm, the next she was pulling a cloak over her head and striding away through the trees, the two wolves following at her heels.

'Where are you going?' he called after her, wondering what had just happened and whether he'd somehow offended her. He hadn't said anything, he was sure of it, and yet something had caused her to shoot up and leave...

What had just happened?

It was several hours before he realised she wasn't coming back.

Chapter Four

Sissa fitted an arrow to her bow, drew back the string, aimed and let go. There was a faint whooshing sound followed by a thud as it slammed into a tree behind the deer, who immediately took off in the opposite direction. Stars! She rolled her eyes at her own lack of focus. It had been an easy shot, but she hadn't been able to hunt during the past few days while she'd been nursing the stranger and her own rumbling stomach had distracted her.

That was the *only* reason for her distraction, she told herself. Hunger. That was all. It *definitely* had nothing to do with an injured warrior with thick, shoulder-length, blond hair and arm muscles the same width as her waist…

She shook her head, wading through the damp undergrowth towards the river, relieved to find that one of her nets had been successful. At least she'd have something substantial to eat tonight. Deftly, she emptied the contents and then made her way back to her roundhouse in the forest clearing, singing an old, half-remembered tune as she went. Being in the company of the warrior—Danr, he'd called himself—seemed to have loosened her tongue somehow, making her want to sing again. It felt strange, but surprisingly good, to fill her lungs with fresh mountain air that tasted even better after the rain, clean and fresh and restorative somehow.

She dropped the salmon beside the fire pit and went into her roundhouse for a cauldron, then along to the stream on the mountainside for some water, still singing. Idly, she wondered where the warrior was now. She'd left him his sword as well as a few supplies so that he'd be free to leave the shelter as soon as he felt well enough—which would probably be soon if he hadn't gone already. He'd been much stronger when she'd left him that morning and there had been nothing wrong with his legs. Or with his mouth either. She hadn't heard so many words put together in years. The people who came to her needing help or medicine never said any more than was necessary, as if her silence were somehow contagious, and it was an arrangement that suited her. Silence was her best protection. It made people afraid of her and people who were afraid left her in peace. *That* was the way she wanted and needed it to be. She would help them and heal them, but that was all. She would never live with or be one of them again. Her old life was over and there was no going back.

But then *he'd* come along. The warrior had talked to her as if he wasn't afraid of her, as if he'd seen her as some kind of *normal* woman. She'd thought him good looking enough when he was unconscious, but awake there was a kind of mesmerising quality about him that drew the eye and held it. The way he'd looked at her when she'd woken up after taking shelter from the rain had made her feel uncharacteristically breathless and dazed, too. It had been a new, almost pleasurable sensation, but one she couldn't and wouldn't allow. It was too unnerving. *He* was too unnerving. And so she'd left, checking his wound one last time before walking away without a backward glance.

At least she was home and safe again now, she thought with a sigh, hooking the metal cauldron on to a tripod above the fire pit, then cutting up a few turnips and adding them to the water. Some wild garlic might be good for her stew, too, she decided, half-turning towards her roundhouse and then stiffening at the sound of Tove's growl. Instantly she whipped around, following the direction of the wolf's gaze towards the trees. Branches were rustling and swaying as if something large were coming towards them, though whatever it was, it didn't seem to have the slightest idea about stealth.

Quickly, she reached for the spear she always kept close at hand and drew her arm back ready to throw. It could be a bear or a rival wolf or…*him*?

She almost dropped the spear again, forgetting to guard her expression for a few seconds as she gaped at the warrior with surprise, closely followed by horror. He'd fastened his sword belt back on and the fur she'd left him was draped around his shoulders, exacerbating his rugged, hirsute appearance. But most bizarre of all was the smile spreading over his face, making his teeth flash white against his sun-bronzed skin, as if he were genuinely pleased to see her again. What was he doing there? Why hadn't he left? How had he found her?

'There you are!' His voice held a note of triumph. 'I might not be able to fight for a while, but I can still track.'

Trembling, she lifted a hand, pointing back in the direction from which he'd emerged. How *dared* he intrude upon her clearing! This was her *home*, hers and Tove's and Halvar's! *Nobody* came here! The people from the village who needed her help knew better than to come so close. She didn't want anyone else here, *especially* not a warrior who seemed twice as big now that he was back on his feet. Warriors destroyed things! They were monsters, not men, killing and burning and plundering wherever they went! Every instinct told her to scream and yell at him to go, but all she could do was point.

'I'm afraid I can't.' His tone was apologetic as he dropped to one knee in a supplicatory gesture. 'I owe you a debt for saving my life and I need to repay it. I still have one good arm and I'll do whatever you ask, any tasks you need doing. I'll even hunt if you want.' He glanced down at his bandage and gave a lopsided grin. 'Just maybe not deer. Not yet. Maybe mice?'

She kept on staring at him, aghast. The words suggested he intended to stay with her for a while, but how was it repaying her when she didn't *want* anything from him, except for him to go away?

'I won't disturb you. I'll build another shelter.' He shuffled closer, ignoring Tove's warning growl. Where was Halvar? Sissa glanced around, but the male wolf was lying off to one side, seemingly unperturbed by the whole scene. Briefly she considered whistling for Tove to attack on her own, but the warrior still had a sword and she dared not take the risk of her companion being injured.

'I'm not a bad cook either.' He stopped beside the fire pit and gestured towards the salmon. 'I can prepare that for you, if you like. What is it? Fish stew?'

Sissa clenched her fists, willing her features back into the customary stillness she adopted around people, but it was impossible. Her whole body was shaking with rage and frustration and the urge to scream at him was too great. She could feel her pulse throbbing in her neck and her head felt as though it was about to burst. If she wasn't mistaken, she could actually hear the blood gushing in angry torrents through her veins. No doubt her face was blazing red. She wouldn't be surprised if her whole body was the same colour.

She threw him one last look of savage fury and stormed into her roundhouse.

Danr looked around for bowls. Cooking the fish hadn't been easy—and that was an understatement. Skinning and deboning a salmon with one good arm had been particularly challenging, especially under the watchful gaze of two large wolves, but he'd finally managed it. As fish stews went, it wasn't too bad either. It could have done with some more flavour, a few herbs perhaps, but whatever other ingredients the woman had, he guessed they were stored inside her roundhouse and he had a feeling that venturing in there would push her temper over the edge.

His arrival had finally penetrated the uncommunicative mask she'd worn so far in all their dealings. He'd actually been taken aback by the expression of outrage on her face when he'd first emerged into the clearing. She might at least have been pleased to see him back on his feet, but she'd looked as if she'd wanted to undo all her hard work and throw her spear at him instead. His attempt to charm her hadn't exactly worked either. The lopsided, self-deprecating smile he'd honed to a fine art over the years rarely failed to convince a woman to do anything, but if one thing was obvious by now it was that *this* woman was different. She wasn't going to leap at the chance of spending more time with him. She wanted him to go.

Unfortunately for her, he couldn't. Even if he went back to his carefully concealed boat, he could hardly row back to the mainland with one arm. And even if he could, Sandulf was in Eireann now, not Alba. What he needed was a place to recuperate, somewhere warm and dry until his arm healed and he was ready to confront Hilda again. Whether this woman liked it or not—and the answer was obviously *not*—he needed her. Now, all he had to do was convince her that she needed him, too.

Doing so, however, was another matter. His offer to work for her hadn't been received very well and she didn't look as though she'd care much about coin, but

surely there was *something* he could offer? If only she
would come out of her roundhouse and talk it would
make negotiating with her a lot easier. Then he could
explain that he meant her no harm and maybe come
to some kind of arrangement. She'd looked as if she'd
been on the verge of saying something earlier, her body
actually trembling with the effort it had cost her to keep
silent, but she'd stopped herself. Why? Why *wouldn't*
she speak to him? He didn't want to upset her any further, but he had the feeling that if he left her to calm
down, she'd simply go back to ignoring him again.
Maybe provoking her was the only way to begin a
conversation...

'The fish is ready,' he called out in the direction of
the roundhouse. It was a curious design, he noticed,
ancient-looking and constructed from wood and turf
in a style he'd never seen before. He presumed it was
Gael, or even Pict, even if she herself looked Norse. 'I
hope you're hungry?'

There was no answer, so he sat down on the ground,
leaning against a tree stump and allowing himself to
relax. He could wait. She couldn't stay in there for ever
and he was the one with the food. All things considered, he felt surprisingly comfortable.

'You know, there are other things I could do for you
besides hunting.' He decided to test how much Norse
she understood. 'I'm very good with my hands. Ask
any woman who's ever met me. They'd all agree, my
hands are practically famous in Maerr.' He fixed his
gaze on the leather curtain over the entrance, watching for any hint of a reaction. 'My mouth, too. That's

probably *more* famous. I can do things with my tongue you can't even imagine.'

There. A small unmistakable twitch of the curtain followed by...stillness again. He sighed and tipped his head back, his mind filled with a startling array of erotic images all of a sudden. Of course, images would be all he would have until he fulfilled his oath, but even if he couldn't actually lie with a woman, there were other things he could do to her, *for* her... Despite his rescuer's spectral appearance, the idea was curiously tempting.

'You know, if you let me, I could think of a hundred different ways to repay you,' he carried on, his body heating at the idea. 'I like exploring a woman's body. I'd start with your breasts.' He closed his eyes, feeling a tightening sensation in his trousers as he imagined the budded peaks of her nipples. 'Then I'd kiss my way down your stomach and over your hips. I'd get to know every part of your body. In detail. Then I'd move down between your legs. I'd taste you there—'

'Stop it!'

He opened his eyes with a jolt, surprised as much by the sound of her voice as the vehemence behind it. He'd been so engrossed in his daydream that it actually took him several seconds to come back to reality, to focus on her livid-looking face as she glared at him from the doorway of her roundhouse.

'You speak Norse!' He felt elated by his success.

'I understand Norse,' she corrected, storming wrathfully towards him. 'I don't speak *anything!*'

'But you are now.'

'Only because you *won't stop*!'

Too late he caught sight of the dagger in her hand, lifting his good arm to block her just as she dropped to a crouching position and held the blade to his throat. The look in her eyes was deadly serious, a raging swirl of storm clouds ready to unleash thunder and lightning.

'I'm sorry.' He lowered his arm again, finally aware he'd gone too far. 'I needed to know if you could understand me.'

'Why?' She seemed to be speaking through clenched teeth, as if it truly cost her to wrench the words out. 'Why did you *need* to? I saved your life! Why come to my home and offer insults in return!'

'I didn't mean it that way.' He glanced down at the dagger and then back up again. 'I'm sorry. I shouldn't have said those things. Forgive me.'

'No.' Her expression was implacable. 'I want you to leave!'

'It's not so easy.'

'Go!'

'Won't you at least tell me your name?'

The question only seemed to make her angrier still. Before he could react, she flipped the dagger around, ramming the hilt hard against his injured arm.

'Go!' She repeated the word more forcefully, ignoring his cry of pain.

'I'm sorry...'

'Do you think just saying so is enough?' She stood up, looming over him the way she had when he'd first seen her, only this time everything about her body was clenched—her jaw, her fists, her muscles—all rigid with tension…

'I don't…' It was becoming harder and harder to speak as his teeth started to chatter. There were white spots dancing before his eyes and he could dimly see a fresh stain of blood spreading through the linen around his arm. 'Please…help me.'

'Save yourself this time.' Her eyes flashed one last time before she turned her back on him. 'You're on your own now, Norseman.'

Chapter Five

Sissa hurled the dagger to the ground and stalked back towards the roundhouse, her throat taut with anger as she wrenched the leather curtain aside and flung herself face-down on to the pile of furs that served as a bed. To her horror, there were tears welling in her eyes.

How *could* he? After everything that she'd done for him, sheltering and feeding and nursing him when he'd been so close to death, was *this* really how he repaid her? With the kind of talk that made her blood run hot and cold at the same time? There were so many conflicting emotions swirling in her chest that she didn't know which was dominant. Anger, confusion, want, need... She felt strung tight, vibrating with all of them at once. She didn't want to think about all the things he'd said he could do to her body either, but when she did... There was an ache in the pit of her stomach and between her thighs that made her insides feel as if they were turning to liquid.

She rolled on to her back, struggling to control the

onslaught of emotion. It had been so long since *anyone* had touched her that just the thought of it was painful. For all her other kindnesses, Coblaith had never held or embraced her, even during the many long nights when she'd cried herself to sleep. The last caress she remembered was the touch of her mother's hand on her cheek...

The tears spilled over, stinging her eyes, coursing down her cheeks and trickling into the furs. The warrior's words had felt cruel, evoking a human connection that she would never, *could* never, have with anyone again. But, worst of all, he'd broken through her defences, provoking her into speech after five years of silence. Combined with her singing earlier, the effort had made her mouth feel stretched and sore, as if her tongue were swollen.

'I'm sorry!' She heard his voice outside again, calling to her. She'd thought—hoped—he'd been on the verge of fainting, but apparently she hadn't hit him hard enough. Did the man *never* shut up?

'I shouldn't have said those things. It was wrong of me,' he called again, as if he truly thought an apology was enough.

She rolled on to her side to watch the leather curtain, inwardly vowing that if he touched as much as a corner then she'd grab the nearest available object—in this case an iron poker beside the hearth—and bring it down over his head.

'What can I do to make things right?'

Fortunately for him, the curtain *didn't* move. Her

itching fingers almost wished it would. The thought of a poker hitting his head was eminently satisfying.

'I already told you to go!' she shouted back. 'I don't *want* you to repay me!'

'That's not the reason.' His voice sounded strained. 'I mean, I want to repay you, but that's not the only reason I can't go.'

'What else can there be?' She felt almost desperate now. 'Why can't you just leave me alone?'

'Because I've nowhere else to go.'

She drew her brows together, rubbing her palms over her cheeks as she considered the words. *Nowhere else to go...* She knew how *that* felt, but it was hard to imagine this warrior not belonging somewhere. Judging by the quality of his mail shirt and weapons, not to mention his arm rings, he was a man of reasonable wealth and standing. How could he *not* belong somewhere? She rolled to a sitting position, took a calming breath, stood up and then stepped back outside. He was sitting on the ground a few feet away, as if he'd staggered so far and then collapsed, ashen-faced and looking as though he were about to vomit. Which might have given her some satisfaction if he hadn't been so close to her roundhouse.

'Here.' She reached for an empty pot and handed it to him. 'Put your head between your legs.'

'Thank you.' He did as she told him, draping his forearms over his knees.

'Don't thank me. I might still hit you again.' She scowled threateningly. 'What do you mean, nowhere else to go? Aren't you one of the new settlers?'

'No. I came from Alba to find someone.' He gave a bitter-sounding laugh. 'As you can see, they weren't very happy to see me.'

'Because you wouldn't stop talking?'

'Something like that.' He looked up again, his lips twitching in a pained kind of smile. 'Perhaps I *should* have kept my mouth shut, but I came here to ask questions, to discover the truth about something that happened three years ago.'

'What something?'

A shadow passed over his face. 'It's a long story.'

'I have time, Norseman.'

'No.' He shook his head. 'I can't talk about it, but I also can't leave until I'm able to do what I came here to get done. It's important.'

'Really?' She pursed her lips. At least she'd found some way to shut him up, but if he wouldn't give her the details then she saw no reason to let him stay. On the other hand, perhaps the words he'd muttered in his sleep were explanation enough...

'How do I know you won't hurt me?' She narrowed her eyes suspiciously. 'I've no idea who you are.'

'I won't hurt you, I swear it. I'm Danr Sigurdsson, bastard son of Jarl Sigurd of Maerr.'

'*Jarl?*'

'I told you, it's a long story. Here.' He unfastened his sword belt and pushed it across the ground to her. 'Take my weapons. If I do anything at all you don't like, then you can set your wolves on me.'

'Aren't you afraid I might anyway?'

'No. You saved my life. That kind of thing makes me trust a person.'

She made a sceptical sound, hardening her heart despite the words. 'Did you come to Skíð alone?'

'Yes. My boat's hidden, but I can't row myself back to the mainland with an injured arm and if I go near a village then the person who did this will find me and finish what they started. They're probably already out looking for me. I need somewhere to shelter until I'm able to defend myself again.' He winced and sucked in a sharp breath. 'Moon's eye, but you have a strong arm, woman.'

'I barely touched you.' She threw a contemptuous glance at the linen binding the poultice. There was a red stain behind it, but not much. The blood looked as if it were already clotting, which meant that whatever damage she'd done was only minor. If what he was saying was true, however, then she could hurt him far more by sending him away. If he couldn't go to one of the villages—and they were still few and far between— then he'd have a hard time surviving on his own and she'd be condemning him to more suffering. Frankly, she might as well not have bothered saving him in the first place. But she was still angry and she still didn't want him there! Of all the people she might have found and helped, why did it have to be a warrior?

'I'm telling the truth, I swear it.' He seemed to sense her hesitation.

She rolled her eyes to the sky and then sniffed the air, her mouth watering suddenly at the scent of his stew. It smelt delicious. Perhaps he hadn't lied about being a good cook, after all. In which case, even if healing him was going to be a longer task than she'd anticipated, perhaps there might be one consolation…

'We should eat,' she said decisively, scooping some of the stew into a bowl and sitting down on the opposite side of the fire pit.

'Does that mean you'll let me stay?' He gave her a searching glance.

'For tonight. Since you cooked.'

'Thank you. And tomorrow, if you let me stay longer, I'll make myself useful. I'll keep out of your way and there'll be no more talk like before, I promise.'

'Good, or I'll cut your arm off next time.' She took a mouthful of stew and then looked up at him in surprise. It tasted even better than it smelled, dissolving in succulent chunks on her tongue. She couldn't imagine what he'd done to it, especially considering the paucity of the ingredients, but she hadn't tasted anything so good since…she couldn't remember when.

'What do you think?' He was watching her eagerly, she realised, as if he were actually keen to hear her opinion.

'Not bad.' She refused to compliment him. 'But I still don't want you here, Norseman.'

'I know.'

'I don't like people, especially warriors. That's why I live alone.'

'I understand, but…' he spread his hands out in appeal '…please?'

'I'll think about it.' She ladled out another spoonful, picked up his sword belt and started towards her roundhouse. 'You can sleep beside the fire tonight. It's not going to rain.'

'Thank you. I appreciate it.'

'Hmm.' She ignored his words of gratitude, whistling for Tove and Halvar to follow her instead. Tove got up obediently, but Halvar only lifted his head briefly before lowering it back on to his paws.

'Is he going to sleep out here, too?' The warrior sounded faintly concerned.

'It looks that way.' She stopped in her doorway and shrugged. 'If you don't like it, you know what you can do.'

'I need logs.' Sissa dropped an axe on to the ground beside the warrior Danr's head. It landed with a satisfyingly loud thump, startling him awake.

'What? What's happening?' He shot upright, reaching for his absent sword, and then groaned at the manoeuvre.

'Logs,' she repeated, refusing to show any sign of sympathy. If he really wanted to stay then she had no intention of making life easy for him. Quite the opposite, in fact, no matter how handsome he looked, with his blond hair sticking out at wild angles around his ridiculously sculpted cheekbones. And how was it possible to have eyes quite *so* blue and piercing? 'See that pile of branches over there? They need chopping into logs. Do you think you can manage that?'

'If that's what you want.' He blinked a few times, as if he were still trying to wake up. 'It might take me a little longer than usual, but I'll get it done.'

'Good, but first you can wash. You smell terrible.'

'And good morning to you, too…' he lifted his left shoulder and sniffed '…although you might have a point.'

'I'm surprised Halvar could bear to sleep so close to you.' She glared at the wolf who only stood up, yawned and stretched.

'Is that what you call him, Halvar?'

'Yes. It means guardian of the rock. He came down from the mountain a year ago, so it seemed fitting.'

'Well, *I* might smell, but he's loud.' Danr chuckled. 'I never knew that wolves snored.'

'Aren't you afraid of him?' She looked between the pair of them curiously. 'Most people are terrified by his size.'

'So was I to begin with, but I decided that if he was going to eat me then he would probably have done it by now.'

'Maybe he's not hungry yet.'

'Ah, well, time will tell, I suppose.'

She lifted an eyebrow, irritated by his cheeriness. 'You know, he's only using you to make a point.'

'Really?' He looked interested. 'What point?'

'That he's only here under protest. Tove is his mate. If he had his way, they'd go off into the forest together.'

Hearing her name, the female wolf emerged from the roundhouse, looked around suspiciously for a few moments, then trotted across the clearing to nuzzle Halvar's nose.

'I see what you mean.' Danr grinned. 'Why won't she go with him?'

'Because I raised her from a cub and she's loyal to me. She knows I'd be all alone if she left.' Sissa bit her lip on the last words. They were more revealing than she'd intended.

'So he's jealous of you?'

'Perhaps.' She tossed her head. 'But mostly he's sulking. *That's* the only reason he stayed with you last night. It's probably why he didn't eat you either.'

Danr reached out and placed a hand tentatively on Halvar's neck, tickling him behind his ears. 'Well, never mind that, we can still be friends, can't we, boy?'

Sissa clenched her jaw, annoyed that the wolf wasn't ripping his arm off. Halvar didn't often let *her* touch him, let alone anyone else, but now his eyes were half-closed as if he were actually enjoying the attention.

'Why is your hair wet?' Danr asked suddenly, as if he'd only just noticed her appearance.

'Because I've been bathing. There's a gorge through those trees where several streams run together.'

'Isn't the water cold?'

'It's come down from the mountain. Of course it's cold.' She threw him a withering look along with a blanket. 'Use this to dry yourself afterwards and hang it up when you're finished.' She pointed towards a length of cord tied between two trees. 'You'll need to wash your clothes, too.'

'I would.' He glanced up at the sky dubiously. 'Only I doubt they'll dry in this weather and I don't have anything else to wear. I dropped my pack somewhere in the forest.' He made a face. 'I'm afraid it's either a bad smell or the sight of me chopping wood naked, which

I'm disinclined to do with an injured arm. Mistakes could be made.'

'Oh, by the stars...'

Sissa rolled her eyes and went back inside the round-house, rummaging in one of her coffers until she found an old pair of trousers and tunic. They hadn't been worn in so long that the wool smelt faintly musty, but it was still a better alternative than smelling him. As for seeing him naked... She shook her head before her imagination ran riot.

'Here.' She carried the clothes back outside and dropped them in front of him. 'You can wear these. They belonged to someone I once knew,' she added when he looked at her enquiringly.

'I see.' He looked as if he were stopping himself from asking more. 'In that case, I appreciate your letting me borrow them.'

'Hmm. Try not to get your shoulder wet.'

'Whatever you say. Wash, change, hang clothes, chop wood.' He gave her a hopeful look. 'Does this mean I can stay for a while?'

'It means you can stay for today. And when you're finished with all that, you can collect some more branches, but not from around here. Go deeper into the forest.' She picked up a basket and reached for her spear. 'I'll be back later with food. You can cook again.'

'With pleasure.' He threw his fur blanket aside and stood up. 'What about the wolves?'

'They go wherever they want.' She arched an eyebrow. 'But that won't bother you, will it? Since you're such *good friends* now...'

'So we are.' He tipped his head, acknowledging the hit.

'But you can have your sword back.' She gestured to where she'd left his sword belt outside the round-house. 'Since there are other dangers in the forest. Just know that if you use a weapon on one of my wolves, I'll kill you myself.'

'Understood.' He nodded. 'Although you still haven't told me your name...?'

She hesitated, her gaze latching on to his for a few seconds. He was smiling the same lopsided smile he'd worn yesterday. It made her chest feel oddly tight and tremulous, as if just the sight of it had some power to constrict her breathing, although something about it struck her as a little too practised. She had the feeling that he knew exactly what effect it caused. The sight of his bare chest where his tunic hung open wasn't exactly helping either. It would have been easier if either his face or physique had been a little less eye-catching, but they were both equally impressive. Even with an arm's length between them she was altogether too aware of him, of his broad shoulders, his musky scent, his powerful abdominal muscles, the sprinkling of pale hair over his chest... But he'd asked her a question, hadn't he? Something about her name?

No, she hadn't told him her name. She hadn't heard it spoken aloud for so long that it seemed to belong to another lifetime. The last person who'd called her by her name had been her mother, her beautiful, grey-eyed mother who'd held her close and then told her to run just minutes before a warrior had cut her down in cold blood… *A warrior*! The tremulous feeling faded, replaced by a block of cold stone.

'No, I didn't.' She turned towards the forest. 'Pick one. I don't care.'

Chapter Six

'Erika!' Danr rubbed the small of his back, aiming another of his lop-sided grins at the woman when she returned to the clearing a few hours later. The sun was a long way past its zenith and he'd been starting to wonder whether something had happened to her. Other than that concern, however, he'd had an unexpectedly enjoyable day—in an exhausting kind of way. It hadn't been easy, but it had made a refreshing change. Most of the time these days, his mind was consumed with thoughts of revenge and retribution, but today the fresh air and physical activity had distracted him. It had felt good to take his mind off Hilda and Joarr for a while. It had actually felt good to be alive, too. It was the first time in three years that he'd thought so—another reason that he hoped the woman would let him stay longer. It was surprising how *much* he wanted to…

'Erika?' She tipped her head to one side with a confused expression.

'That's what I've decided to call you. Don't you like it? Because I'm still toying with Bersa.'

'Hmm.' She made a face and dropped a pair of trout on to the ground. 'Dinner.'

'Ah, fish are my specialty. What's all that?' He peered into her basket, intrigued to see an assorted collection of plants and fungus. 'Food or medicine?'

'A little of both. Now where are my logs?'

'Over there.' He gestured proudly towards a stack of wood so high it was almost teetering, pleased to see her look of surprise.

'That's more than I expected.'

'Good.' Because he'd almost broken his other arm trying to prove how useful he could be. 'Do I get a smile as a reward?'

'No.' She gave him a narrow-eyed look instead. 'We'd better store them somewhere dry while we can.'

'In the roundhouse?'

'No.' She didn't explain, just took her basket inside and came back with a leather hide. As he watched, she placed a few of the logs on top, then folded the ends over and dragged it behind her through the trees.

Perplexed, Danr scooped a few more logs under his good arm and followed, Tove and Halvar scampering ahead towards the craggy edge of the mountain. Despite the recent snow, the weather had warmed up during the day, making the air feel almost balmy by comparison. There were signs of impending winter everywhere and yet he could almost have believed it was summer again. The late afternoon sky was turning from blue to orange, burnishing the tops of the

trees with gold so it seemed as though they glowed.
Now that he looked closer he could see lots of different kinds growing together—pine, mostly, as well as
birch and alder and a few oak. They looked beautiful, less stark and menacing now than when he'd first
found himself lost in the forest. The atmosphere was
reassuringly peaceful, too, the silence disturbed only
by the chirruping of birds, the whistle of the breeze
in the canopy and the sound of logs being dragged in
front of him. At that moment, he could almost forget
why he'd come to Skíð in the first place.

They walked uphill for several minutes before the
woman stopped and started wrenching at what looked
like undergrowth, but turned out to be a screen made
of interwoven branches and bracken covering a gap in
the mountainside.

'I store the things I can't keep in the roundhouse
here,' she told him, ducking under a rocky overhang
and disappearing into the darkness.

'Impressive.' Danr ducked, too, and then stood up
beside her, his voice echoing around a large granite
chamber. He stared in amazement, a few more gaps
in the rock higher up allowing in just enough light to
illuminate a range of objects stacked around the walls.
Piles of furs and leathers, pots and pans…even a pair
of chests and a peg loom in one corner. He wondered
where she'd got it all from, living alone in the wilderness. Had she stolen it? Or were they family heirlooms?

She'd said that the clothes he was wearing had belonged to *someone* she once knew and the fact that
she *could* speak suggested she'd spent some of her life

around people. *Norse* people, too, since her accent was that of a native. What had happened to them? Why was she on her own now? The more he knew about her, the more of a mystery she seemed to become.

'Are all of these things yours?'

'Yes.' She dragged the logs to one corner and tipped them out on to the ground. To his dismay there was already a sizeable amount of firewood. So much for making himself indispensable. She already seemed well equipped for winter. It was becoming increasingly obvious that she could manage perfectly well without him.

'So you just leave everything here?' He noticed several swords and shields propped against one wall. They were *definitely* Norse. 'Aren't you worried about someone finding it all?'

'No. The entrance is hidden and most people don't come up the mountain. They're afraid of Tove and Halvar.' She straightened up, rubbing her hands together briskly before walking slowly towards him. 'And me.'

'You?' He held her gaze in the half-darkness. 'Are *you* dangerous then?'

'Some people think so. They say that I can make storms when the mood is upon me.' She stopped in front of him. 'Maybe you should listen to them and be afraid of me, too.'

'Maybe I should, but I was always too reckless to know what was good for me.' He tried to sound nonchalant, though he had to admit there was something elemental about her appearance at that moment. Her pale hair seemed to shimmer in the faint light, as if it might shoot out silvery sparks at any moment. She was standing so close that he could reach out and touch her if he wanted to—and he wanted to, he realised with a jolt.

'Other people just think I'm mad,' she continued as if he hadn't spoken. 'Maybe they're right and I *am* mad. How would I know if I was?'

Danr drew in a deep breath, taken aback by the intensity of her expression. She looked as if she genuinely wanted an answer, as if she were relying on him to give her one, too, but how could he? He didn't know her. He didn't know if it was even *possible* to know her. She was more inscrutable and mysterious than any woman he'd ever met before. But she was still looking at him...

'Maybe you wouldn't know. Maybe none of us really know ourselves,' he answered, rubbing a hand over his chin before gesturing around the cave. 'Personally, however, I think you're too well organised to be mad.'

'Perhaps I ought to summon a storm to convince you.'

'Ah, but you already did that, remember? You summoned a snowstorm when you first found me. I know that was you...' He swayed slightly towards her, lowering his voice to an undertone. 'You might be a mystery, Erika or Bersa or whatever you want me to call you, but you're not mad. I think you're just very good at pretending.'

Her eyes widened for a moment, flickering over him as if she were seeing him properly for the first time.

'Danr Sigurdsson...' She said his name softly, yet in

a way that seemed to echo all around the cave. 'You're not like other warriors.'

'No?' The words came too close for comfort. 'Do you know so many then?'

The question made her gaze dip briefly. 'I may live alone, but I have eyes and ears and I know the way they behave.'

'You mean the Norse in the village or the Gaels?'

'The Gaels have moved inland. There's only Norse on this side of the island now.'

'And only one Norse village in this part of the island.'

'True. You look like them, but you're different.'

'Maybe because I'm a warrior who can't fight, for a few weeks anyway. I don't know what that makes me.' He smiled and shrugged his shoulders, trying to make light of it. 'Except for your servant and cook.'

'No…' She didn't react to the gesture, only studying him a bit longer. 'I think you must always have been different.'

The smile fell from his face. *Different.* An outsider. A bastard son to a king with three good, strong, legitimate sons… The old pang of bitterness hit him harder than usual. Even though he'd had Rurik, he'd always been aware of the difference between them and their half-brothers, having to fight for every scrap of their father's attention, having to prove they were worthy to be in his hall alongside warriors like Brandt and Alarr. He'd done his best to bury and hide his feelings, to conceal his sense of not belonging behind a careless, mocking exterior, yet somehow this woman had seen

straight through him, right through to his core. It was
a disconcerting sensation. Women were rarely interested in anything more than his face.

'I just talk more than most warriors.' He forced a
smile back to his lips. 'My brothers always said so.'

'Mmm.' Her gaze turned inwards. 'It feels strange
to talk again. It's been so long.'

'How long have you been alone?' He quirked an
eyebrow, glad of the change in subject.

'Long enough.'

'Without anyone to talk to?' It was hard to believe
that a person would choose to live that way. 'It sounds
lonely.'

'Sometimes it is.'

'Don't you get frightened, living out here with only
animals for company? Why not go to one of the villages? Surely the people there would value a healer?'

'Because they aren't the people I *want* to be with.'
Her eyes shot back to his, brighter than before. 'Those
people are gone and I don't want anything to do with
any others. Villages aren't safe either. I've seen men
behave much worse than animals. People are dangerous. They can't be trusted. Warriors especially.'

'You mean your village wa—?'

'So, Danr Sigurdsson,' she interrupted before he
could finish his question, 'you come to Skíð on your
own, you almost get yourself killed, then you refuse
to leave. Either you're the one who's mad or you're just
stubborn. Which is it?'

'A little of both, maybe.' He straightened his shoulders. 'All I know is that I came here for a purpose and I'm going to fulfil it, no matter what.'

She moved even closer, until they were standing toe to toe and chest to chest, leaving only a sliver of air between them. 'Does it mean so much to you, this truth you came here to find?'

'It's all I care about now.'

'More than your life?'

'My life...' He knitted his brows together. This wasn't a subject he wanted to talk about, especially not to a stranger—a woman!—but the words seemed to be coming of their own accord. 'My life never had much meaning. Doing what I came here for is the only thing that might give it some value.'

There was a long, drawn-out moment of silence while she stared up at him, so intently he had the feeling she was trying to see all the way to the back of his skull. He had the unnerving suspicion she might actually be able to do it, too. For a woman who'd barely looked him in the eye to begin with, she had an extremely disconcerting stare. He felt as if he were being stripped naked.

'All right.' She nodded her head finally. 'You can stay until your arm heals, but you do what I say, you build your own shelter and you keep out of my roundhouse.'

'Understood.'

'And *when* you leave, you don't mention anything about this or me to anyone. You don't make me regret helping you.'

'Not a word.'

'Then we have an agreement, Danr Sigurdsson.'

'And you have my thanks.'

She gave an infinitesimal nod of the head. 'In that case, you need your rest. You can bring the rest of the logs tomorrow.'

'I can do it tonight.'

'No. You promised to do whatever I said and I'm telling you to rest and heal.' Her eyes narrowed again. 'The sooner you do that, the sooner you can leave me alone.'

'Then your wish is my command.' He felt curiously touched by the words. 'Thank you, lady.'

Chapter Seven

Sissa tied a knot of yarn to the shaft of her drop spindle and started to spin, looking up every so often as Danr stirred yet more ingredients into the cauldron beside him. They'd had a busy day. She'd done some weaving on a hand loom while he'd taken the rest of the logs to the cave, then washed some clothes and completed half-a-dozen other tasks she'd given him. She'd deliberately made no allowances for his arm, yet he'd done everything without complaint, even entertaining her while they'd carded wool with a story about a dragon and a beautiful maiden who was rescued by a brave warrior.

The time had passed quickly since it was hard to imagine a skald telling it better. After such a long day, she would have expected him to be surly and exhausted, but he seemed to have endless reserves of energy and good humour. The more he'd talked, the more words had started coming back to her, too, as if some long-dormant part of herself had awoken again. She'd wanted to applaud when his story was over, although she hadn't since that might have implied she was actually enjoying his company. None the less, she had to admit he was nothing like she'd expected a warrior to be. He was also more than a handsome face—funny, charming and apparently interested in cooking. She'd never seen so much fuss over what was, as far as she could tell, essentially just nettle soup. At that moment, he wasn't even talking, utterly engrossed in the cauldron in front of him.

'How many more ingredients can it possibly need?' she asked finally. 'How long until we can actually eat it?'

'*Patience*, Erika-Bersa. It'll be ready when it's ready.' He clucked his tongue, dipping his spoon into the bubbling liquid and then winking across the fire pit. '*Now* it's ready.'

'Thank goodness.' She dropped her gaze, alarmed by a swooping sensation in her abdomen. It had happened that morning when he'd winked at her, too, although she had no idea why. Not that it was *un*pleasant, but it seemed to add an atmosphere of tension to the air around them. Or maybe she was the only one who felt it?

'It just needs to cool for a little while.' He removed the cauldron from the tripod and set it aside, swatting at a small, winged insect as he sat down again. 'I hope you're hungry.'

'Ravenous. Here.' She put her spindle aside and reached into her basket, tossing him a small bundle that he caught in mid-air.

'Bog myrtle?'

'It helps to keep insects away. Tuck it behind your ear or they'll go for your neck.'

'You want me to put plants in my hair?' He looked sceptical for a moment and then did as she suggested. 'Well, it's worth a try, I suppose. I'm tired of being eaten.' He grinned suddenly. 'At least I know you won't tell anyone.'

'Very funny.' She fought to repress a smile. With a green sprig behind his ear he looked even less like a warrior. 'Do you *really* like cooking?'

'Yes. I like good food, good clothes and good f—' He bit his tongue abruptly. 'A few other things.'

'Fighting?' She pursed her lips, trying to remind herself that he *was* still a warrior. 'How many battles have you been in, Norseman?'

'*Danr*, and more than I care to remember.'

'Do you *like* fighting?'

'I like wielding a sword. I like the discipline, the skill…'

'The killing?'

'No.' His expression darkened. 'I never enjoy that. Some men might, but I don't.'

'Then why do it? Power? Land?'

He heaved a sigh. 'There are lots of reasons for fighting, some better than others. Sometimes it's a matter of survival, sometimes honour, sometimes it's to hold on to what's yours, but to take another man's life…it's a terrible thing.'

'What about women? Families?'

'No!' A muscle clenched in his jaw. 'I would never harm innocents.'

'Some warriors do.'

'Then maybe I *am* a different kind of warrior after all.'

She held on to his gaze for a few seconds and then reached for her bowl. The tone of his voice was angry, as if he really meant what he was saying. As if some warriors *were* different, as if *he* really was… She took a mouthful of soup and then blinked.

'This is delicious.'

'You needn't sound so surprised. You've enjoyed everything else I've cooked, haven't you?'

'Yes, but this is nettle soup. I've made it a hundred times, but it's never tasted like this.' She tipped her head to one side, regarding him as if he were some kind of new species. 'How did you learn to cook like this?'

'There was an old woman who lived with us when I was a boy. I was talkative even back then, but she listened to me. One day I asked her to teach me, so she did.' He shrugged. 'I used to cook for my mother. It was one of the few ways I could please her.'

'Your mother?' She couldn't resist asking. He'd said something about being a bastard… 'Where is she now?'

'She *was* in Maerr, but she died. Sixteen years ago.'

'I'm sorry.' She paused briefly before curiosity got the better of her again. 'What was she like?'

'Raven-haired and beautiful.' His expression warmed though there was a faint look of anguish in his eyes, too. 'Her name was Saorla and she was the sister of an Irish king—or so we recently discovered. My father met her when he was a young man and carried her away with him when he left. Of course he promised her everything, his love and devotion as well as a life of comfort and riches in his kingdom of Maerr. What he *didn't* tell her was that he already had a wife.'

'You mean he lied to her?'

'Blatantly, yes.' His jaw muscles tightened again. 'So having shamed and humiliated her, he made her his concubine instead.' He reached down and picked up a twig, using it to draw a pattern in the dirt. 'My father was a great warrior and Jarl, but where women were concerned, he wasn't a good man. He only thought of himself. My mother learnt that the hard way.'

'Why didn't she go back to Eireann?'

'At first because she had no way to get there. Then my brother Rurik and I were born and we bound her to Maerr for ever.' He threw the twig away with a grimace. 'So she made the best of a bad situation.'

She blinked. 'That seems a strange way to think of yourself.'

'It's only the truth. She did her best for us, but she was never happy. As for our father, she loved *and* hated him, I think, and who could blame her? Most of the time they just argued.'

'You weren't close to her, then?'

'Rurik was always closer to her in looks and appearance, whereas I...well, I took after our father. It made things difficult. In any case, she died of a fever when Rurik and I were eight and after that we moved into our father's hall.'

'Rurik...' The name was familiar. 'You spoke of him before.'

'What?' His brows snapped together. 'When?'

'When you were unconscious. You said other names, too, but he was the one you mentioned the most.'

'He's my twin. We have three half-brothers we're close to as well, but with Rurik it's different.' He reached for his soup with a frown. '*Was* different.'

'What do you mean?'

'He married last winter. Now he lives in Glanno-venta and thinks the sun rises and sets in his wife's eyes.'

'Is that so bad?'

'No. He and Annis are perfect for each other and they deserve to be happy after everything they've been through. It's just hard not to be...'

'Jealous?'

'No!' he answered too quickly and then pulled a face. 'Maybe a little. Rurik was the one person I could always talk to about anything. He was the only one who understood what it was like to not really belong either. Our father recognised us as his sons, but we were still bastards. Neither of our parents particularly wanted us. Now Rurik's found a place where he *can* belong—someone else to belong with, too. I suppose a part of me is jealous.' He shook his head. 'I'm not proud of the fact.'

'At least you know he's safe and happy. When you love someone, that's the most important thing, surely?'

'I suppose so.' He looked up from his soup, studying her so intently for a moment that she found herself dipping her head to avoid his gaze.

'So you moved into your father's hall when you were eight and that was the end of cooking?' She hastened to change the subject.

'Yes. Jarls' sons don't become cooks.' He sounded matter of fact about it. 'Or skalds for that matter. So I learned to become a warrior instead. A good one.' He glanced down at his arm. 'Most of the time anyway. *This* was a mistake. I was foolish and let emotion get the better of me. It won't happen again.'

'Maybe you just shouldn't fight again.' She gave him a pointed look. 'I didn't save your life so you could go and get yourself killed afterwards—or kill someone else, for that matter.'

'I don't want to kill anyone, believe me, but I still need answers.'

'Then maybe you should think of another way to get them.'

They lapsed into silence while they ate, the skies gradually darkening around them until finally Danr leaned back, rolled his shoulders and sighed.

'Do you know what we need? A game.'

'What?' She finished her last spoonful of soup. 'What kind of game?'

'*Tafl?*' He gestured in the direction of the cave. 'Do you have a board stored away somewhere?'

'No. Who would I play with?'

'Good point. All right, then, we'll improvise.' He reached down and picked up some twigs. 'Knuckle bones. Or knuckle sticks in this case.'

He threw the twigs up into the air, watching as they fell and then catching as many as he could on the back of his hand.

'Four.' He made a disparaging face. 'I haven't played in a while. It works better with bones.'

'I used to play it like this.' She found a smooth, grey stone, tossing it up and then picking up as many twigs as she could from the ground before catching the stone again. 'Nine.' She threw him a look of triumph.

'All right.' He did the same thing. 'Ha! Nine as well. We're even.'

'Not until I've had another turn.'

'Then let's make this interesting, shall we? Ten turns each. The winner gets a prize.'

'What kind of a prize?' She folded her arms suspiciously.

'That depends. If I win, you have to tell me something about yourself.'

'I said you could only stay if you didn't ask me questions.'

'But this is a game. It's different. And if you win, you get something *you* want. The only condition is that you have to use your left hand, too. That's only fair.'

'All right…' She pursed her lips, considering her prize. 'Another story.'

'Really?' He looked pleased. 'You enjoyed my story before?'

'It passed the time.'

'Ah… Well then, I'm glad I could help. Now do we have a challenge?'

'We do.' She nodded and flexed her fingers. 'I'll go first.'

They played for several minutes, keeping a tally with marks on the ground, Sissa leading at first, then Danr, until it all came down to the final round.

'And the Norseman wins!' Danr whooped in celebration as he beat her by two twigs.

'All right.' She chewed on her bottom lip, suddenly anxious about what she'd agreed to. 'What do you want to know?'

'Mmm.' He scratched his chin thoughtfully, prolonging the moment. 'Your roundhouse, it's not built in a style I recognise. Did you build it?'

Was that it? She almost sagged with relief at the question, glad it wasn't anything more personal.

'No, it's an old Pictish design. It was here when I came, though I've made repairs over the years.'

'So it was empty when you found it?'

'No.' She hesitated briefly. '*I* was found. You aren't the only one who was rescued from the forest.'

'You were rescued?' He sounded intrigued. 'What happened?'

She shook her head. 'You've had your question.'

'But it led to another one. Do I need to challenge you again?'

'No.' She yawned. 'I'm too tired.'

'Then you leave me no choice but to make it up.' He sat down on the tree stump, drumming his fingers on his knees until he snapped them together abruptly. 'I've got it. You were found by a powerful sorceress who bound you to silence. The spell could only be broken by the arrival of a hand—'

'Handsome warrior?' she finished for him. 'Do all your stories involve handsome warriors?'

'Not *all*...' he gave his lopsided grin '...but most of them, yes.'

'Stars!' She rolled her eyes. 'Stop doing that!'

'What? I thought you said you liked my stories.'

'I said they passed the time, but I meant stop smiling like that.'

He quirked an eyebrow. 'You want me to stop smiling?'

'No, just stop smiling like *that*. It looks as if you're trying to persuade me to do something.'

'I am. I want you to tell me who found you in the forest.'

'Just smile normally. Be yourself.'

He blinked as if the idea were new to him, then looked her straight in the eye and curved his lips. 'Like this?'

'Much better.' She nodded with approval.

'Good enough for you to tell me who found you?'

'Oh, all right.' Her lips twitched despite herself. 'Her name was Coblaith, but she was no sorceress. She was a Gael, a healer, and after she rescued me she brought me to live here. We spoke different languages, so we communicated through gestures instead. I suppose I got out of the habit of talking, but she still taught me all about herbs and how to use them. If it hadn't been for her, I would probably have died.'

'So she found you all alone in the forest?'

'Yes.'

'Completely alone?' He was silent for a moment. 'What happened to her?'

'She was already old when she found me. Already weakening, too, I think. Then one morning she started up the mountain on her own without a cloak or a stick or anything. I went to go with her, but she just gestured for me to stay. She gave me this.' She touched her fingers to the torc around her neck. 'I don't know how she found the strength to climb up there, but she did. I never saw her again after that.'

'And you've lived here ever since?'

'Yes. It's been five winters since she found me. Three since she left.'

'Three winters on your own?'

She nodded and lapsed into silence, surprised by her own words. She'd just told him more about herself than she'd ever intended to, but something about him encouraged confidence. Even so, it had to stop now. He hadn't asked what had happened to her family, but she could sense the question hovering in the air between them.

'Where's your shelter?'

'Mmm?' He gave a small start, as if she'd just interrupted some chain of thought. 'Oh, over there.' He pointed towards a corner of the clearing.

'Where?' She peered closer at a pile of branches she'd assumed he'd gathered together for firewood. 'You mean *that*?'

'Yes. In my defence, I didn't have much time.'

'Obviously.' She tried to keep a straight face and couldn't, a peal of laughter bubbling up before she could stop it. Danr paused in the act of reaching for the cauldron to look at her, his expression arrested, before he laughed, too, his blue eyes sparkling into hers.

'I'm glad my efforts amuse you.' He spoke in a tone of mock indignation.

'I'm sorry. It's a good start, but…'

'It's terrible?'

'Yes!' Another burst of giggles erupted.

'I think this is the first time I've seen you smile.' He put a hand up quickly. 'That doesn't mean you have to stop.'

'But I do.' She put a hand on her stomach. 'It hurts. Wait here…' She went into her roundhouse and came back again with a leather pelt. 'You can drape this on top. It should keep off the worst of the drizzle as long as there's no wind.'

'You think it's going to rain?' He glanced up at the sky. 'It doesn't look like it to me.'

'Trust me, it'll rain before morning. Maybe not much, but there'll be another downpour again soon. You'll need to build something more substantial beforehand.'

'Maybe you could give me some advice?'

'Maybe. Here.' She held out the pelt and then inhaled sharply as their fingers inadvertently brushed against, then wrapped around each other at the same moment as their eyes met and held, a hot searing sensation like a flash of lightning passing between them. Warmth coiled in her stomach and her heart gave a sudden, unexpected lurch before she jerked away.

'Thank you.' His voice sounded rougher than before. 'I seem to be saying that a lot.'

'Yes.' She twisted her face to one side, too disturbed by their touch to look at him any longer. For a brief moment, all of her consciousness had seemed to hone in on that one spot, on the heat and pressure of his skin against hers. Her fingers still felt as though they were tingling. Somehow his touch had set fire to her blood, making her knees feel alarmingly unsteady, as if they might give way and drop her straight into his arms at any second. The very idea made her take a step backwards. The last thing she wanted was to get any closer to him, but it was becoming impossible to deny the effect he had on her.

She risked a quick peek sideways again and found him staring back, his gaze heated though he was wearing an expression of intense puzzlement. There was a crease between his brows, too, as if he were trying to make sense of something. Whatever it was, it made her nerves hum and her heart thud heavily against her ribcage. If she wasn't mistaken, there was even gooseflesh on her arms, though she wasn't remotely cold. None of which she wanted him to know about.

'You know, I can't keep on calling you Erika-Bersa.' His gaze seemed to darken the longer he looked at her. 'You could at least choose one or the other.'

'No.' She gave a small cough and whistled for Tove. 'I told you, I don't care. Now you should get some sleep. There are more jobs for you to do tomorrow.'

Danr pressed his hands against his knees, watching as Erika-Bersa walked with long, purposeful strides towards the roundhouse. He felt very aware of his surroundings all of a sudden, of the crackle and hiss of the fire, of the scorching heat that seemed to have just flared out of it, of the strange absence of breeze in the air and the almost uncanny stillness of the trees around them. Most of all he was aware of her, his nerves attuned to every movement she made. It was a long time since he'd been aware of *any* woman. Now he wondered if she'd been as aware of him as he'd been of her. Her abrupt departure made him suspect that she had.

It had been an enjoyable evening after another enjoyable day. He'd been feeling somewhat triumphant, too, since he'd finally succeeded in coaxing a smile out of her. Laughter even. It had been like a burst of sunshine, more dazzling and rewarding than just about any smile he'd ever seen before. They'd established a friendship of sorts, too, even if he *still* didn't know her name. He'd thought about asking her this as his prize, except that he'd had a feeling that doing so would have disturbed the new harmony between them. It seemed bizarre to keep calling her Erika-Bersa, but if that was what she wanted then it would have to do.

He got up and hauled the pelt over his makeshift shelter. It felt strange spending time in the company of a woman again, especially such an unusual one. She wasn't like any woman he'd ever spent time with before. She wasn't beautiful or flirtatious. She didn't speak teasing words or give him coy glances. She didn't do anything to attract him, yet all day he'd found himself unable to resist looking at her. She *ought* to have been easy to resist. She was all hard lines and sharp angles, but he still found himself wanting to look at her. Wanting to be close to her, too.

When they'd been playing knuckle sticks he'd actually found himself swaying towards her, just as he had in the cave, his face moving instinctively towards hers as if he wanted to kiss her. He'd pulled away again the moment he'd realised, but he'd had to stop himself several times from doing it again.

As she'd sat beside the fire pit, her grey eyes had looked alluringly smoky, too, deep and mysterious and altogether too dangerous for him to look into for long. Then when their fingers had touched he'd felt a powerful impulse to clasp on to them and hold tight. It was confusing. Of all the women he'd seen over the past three years, she was surely one of the least memorable, and yet she *interested* him. Odder still, she comforted him. Not deliberately, of course—he suspected she would still rather see the back of him—but somehow just by being there. Her very presence was comforting. But it was probably just because she'd saved his life and he felt safe with her, that was all. Maybe there was a mild attraction, mild to moderate even, but that was irrelevant. He had no intention of acting upon it…did he?

No! He frowned at the momentary lapse. Even if he hadn't made an oath, he was in her debt twice over. She'd saved his life *and* she was giving him shelter. He wouldn't repay her with anything less than honourable behaviour. He wouldn't degrade her by thinking of her in that way either. It was already obvious that she was worth ten of him—ten hundred of him. He was only alive because she'd saved and protected him. The best thing he could do now was put all thoughts of her out of his mind and go to sleep—and try very hard not to dream of grey eyes and a wild crown of silver-blonde hair.

Chapter Eight

Danr yawned, stretched and then crawled out from beneath his shelter, relieved that none of the haphazardly arranged branches had collapsed upon him during the night. A thin layer of mist hung over the treetops, chilling the air, coating the branches in dampness and blocking all but the most persistent rays of watery daylight. Just as Erika-Bersa had predicted, the weather had changed again, making it impossible to see beyond the edge of the clearing. It wasn't a particularly promising start to the morning, but perhaps it was a useful jolt back to reality. Despite his best intentions, his dreams had been altogether too lucid and at least the cold was distracting.

He ran his hands over his face, ruffled his hair and then wandered away towards the river to wash. Leaves rustled behind him and he turned to find Halvar following close at his heels. He smiled at the sight. The wolf's large, silent presence reminded him in a funny way of Rurik. He wasn't sure his twin brother would appreciate the comparison, but *he* found it comforting. And there was that word again: *comforting*. Since when had being comforted become so important to him?

'Good morning.' He held out a hand, letting the wolf nudge its wet nose against his wrist. 'You know, I always thought Maerr was a damp place, but I've never seen mists like these. I feel like I'm walking through clouds.' He rubbed his hand over the animal's head and then carried on towards the gorge, yawning a few more times as he descended the slope. 'Is your mistress still sleeping? Then we'll bathe first today, shall we?'

The words had barely left his mouth when he saw her. She was standing straight ahead of him in one of the pools below a small waterfall, hip-deep in water and without as much as a shift to cover her nakedness. She was also, he could see, oblivious to his arrival, which still gave him an opportunity to leave...

He stood immobile, ordering himself to retreat and yet apparently unable to do so. No matter how hard he tried, he couldn't seem to lift either one of his feet off the ground. His eyes were being similarly disobedient, riveted on her slim figure as she crouched down, dipping her whole body under the water for a few seconds, then stood up and tossed her head from side to side, sending a spray of water all the way through the air to his feet.

He swallowed, assailed by a rush of pure lust as she ran her hands through the long, waist-length tresses, wringing out the droplets and then drawing the bulk of it over one shoulder. Her body was just as lean and angular and spear-like as he'd thought the first time he'd seen her, without as much as a hint of any womanly curve, yet now it struck him as the most erotic, enticing figure he'd ever seen.

Moon's eye! He hadn't as much as looked at a woman in three years. There had been opportunities enough, but they'd all left him cold. Whereas now... now he was mesmerised. Why now? Why with *this* woman? He felt as though all the blood in his body had just rushed straight to his groin.

He was still ordering his legs to move when she looked over her shoulder at him, just a brief glance before she bent over, allowing him a tantalising view of her posterior as she scooped some water into her cupped hands and then scrubbed them over her face.

'I'm sorry...' He croaked the words out, though for once he didn't know what else to say. She twisted slightly towards him as if expecting more, but he seemed utterly incapable of further speech. His throat was dry, his groin was painfully hard and his eyes were transfixed by the drops of water pouring in glistening rivulets down her body, over her breasts and towards the crease between her legs... He finally succeeded in dragging his gaze away, half-expecting her to scream at him for staring, but having noted his arrival she didn't seem to be paying him much attention at all, as if she didn't particularly object to his scrutiny either. It was almost too much temptation to bear. He might have preferred it if she'd screamed at him...

'You're awake early,' she said at last, striding out of the water and reaching for a piece of linen hanging from a nearby branch.

'Yes.' He shook his head, trying to think of something else to say. Trying to remember any words at all. 'I thought you were still asleep.'

She shrugged and started to dry herself down with rough, vigorous strokes. Too rough, Danr thought, staring again as he watched the movement of the linen. If she gave it to him, then he could do a *much* better job. He'd soothe her skin instead of turning it red with scrubbing. He'd use his hands and mouth, too, rubbing and licking the moisture away... The idea almost made him groan aloud. Just when he'd thought he couldn't get any harder... The urge to touch her was so great that he had to clench his fists to stop himself reaching out to stroke the side of her hip.

'What is it?' She looked up suddenly, a small crease between her brows. 'Why are you looking at me like that?'

'What?' He jerked his head up quickly. How could he answer that? He was behaving as if he'd never seen a naked woman in his life, like a boy instead of a man with far too many years of experience, while she...well, she was obviously an innocent, even more than he'd suspected. She seemed not to have not the faintest inkling of the effect she was having on him, which was a relief since she'd probably tell him to leave straight away if she did.

'I was just...looking.' He winced inwardly. *Just looking?* They were arguably the most pathetic words he'd ever said to a woman. No attempt at an excuse. Nothing about her beauty or desirability either. *Just looking?*

Fortunately, she seemed not to find anything strange about them, pulling a tunic over her head—thank the stars!—and then striding towards him.

'What are you doing?' He leapt backwards as she lifted a hand towards his injured arm.

'Checking your wound.' She gave him a look that suggested he must have taken a blow to the head. 'The cut should have closed by now.'

'Oh.' He let out a shaky breath. 'Maybe we should do that later. You must be cold.'

'I don't think about the temperature. It's the best way.'

'Really?' He was starting to feel desperate, his own temperature soaring so high he felt as though he were standing next to a bonfire. 'Maybe we should wait a few more days just in case?'

'No. It's time now.'

To his dismay, she reached for his arm again, un-ravelling the bandage and peering at the wound for so long that he wondered if time itself had stopped. His whole body was rigid with tension and his heartbeat was pounding like a drum in his ears, so loudly he was certain she must be able to hear it—which was all right just as long as that was the *only* thing she noticed and she kept her gaze on the upper part of his body...

'*Much* better,' she said finally, running a finger over the line of the cut in a way that made his breath catch and then hiss sharply between his teeth. The sound of it made her head tip to one side. 'Are you all right, Danr?'

Danr? He swallowed another moan. *Of course* she

used his name now! The sound of it on her lips was almost enough to undo him.

'I'm fine.'

'You don't look fine.'

'It's nothing.'

'Did it hurt when I touched you?'

He almost laughed at the question. It was close to torture, but he could hardly say that. 'No.'

'Good. Come with me.'

She took hold of his arm before he could object, leading him towards the pool's edge. He went, grinding his teeth against a powerful urge to catch her up over his shoulder and carry her off to some soft patch of ground instead. In his current condition it would probably mean wrenching his arm from its socket, but it might still be worth it.

'You needn't worry about getting it wet now,' she murmured, scooping some water up and letting it trickle between her fingers over his injury. 'Just don't rub it.'

'I won't.' He wasn't sure what had happened to his voice. It sounded deeper than he'd ever heard it, more like his brother Brandt's than his own.

She looked as if she were about to go, then frowned and lifted a hand to his forehead. 'You look feverish.'

'I'm not.' He clutched at her hand and tore it away from his face, feeling as though he'd just been scolded. Suddenly he was more than eager to plunge himself into a pool of frigid cold water.

'Are you certain?'

'Very.' He attempted to let go of her hand and found

himself rubbing his thumb over the insides of her fingers instead. The calluses there made him want to caress her even more. Damn it, he wanted to do more than that. He wanted to fall on her like a thirsty man might fall on a barrel of mead. If she touched him just one more time, then she might find out just how much… But he was determined to do the right thing, to hold to his oath. It was the thought of that which helped him to release her.

'I'll see you back in the clearing.' He turned and took a few steps away, tearing his tunic off to distract himself with activity. The feeling of cold air on his skin was a relief, cooling his blood and helping his pulse return to normal. He took a deep breath, waiting for her to leave before removing his trousers, but there was no sound of movement. At last he risked turning his head, only to find their positions reversed. She was the one staring at him now, a swathe of colour across her cheeks and throat.

'As you wish,' she said finally, seeming to come back to herself with a jolt before spinning on her heel and walking away.

Sissa glared at her feet as she tripped over a rock on her way back to the roundhouse, almost falling flat on her face. How was *that* possible? She walked along this path every morning. She knew every rock and pebble and even plant along the way. How was it possible for her to forget and stumble?

It was all *his* fault, the man, Danr's. The way he'd stared at her—first when she'd stood dripping wet in the water and then afterwards when she'd been drying—had only reminded her of the evening before and the strange, almost visceral reaction she'd experienced at his touch—a reaction she'd spent half the night convincing herself she'd imagined.

Now just his expression had unsettled her. At first, she'd supposed it was simply surprise at her nakedness, but surely he couldn't have been *that* surprised? Or maybe it was because she'd made no attempt to cover herself? But why would she have? Nakedness was only natural. Animals never worried about showing their bodies. It was only people who acted strangely about them, although she had to admit, his presence had made her feel somewhat self-conscious. She wasn't used to being looked at and even if she had been, Birger had once told her that she had a long face and a skinny body, which was as true now as it had been five years ago. She might have grown taller, but her body had remained as thin as a sapling. Doubtless the Norseman had been thinking the same thing, although his gaze hadn't *seemed* critical. On the contrary, there had been a definite warmth behind it—heat, even. The same heat she'd thought she'd seen in his eyes the evening before. She hadn't known what to think about that, let alone how to react, but the more she'd tried to act naturally, to concentrate on practicalities like inspecting his wound, the stranger his behaviour had become. When she'd touched his arm, his body had gone positively rigid with tension, as if he'd thought she might actually hurt him—as if she'd *already* been hurting him somehow.

The sight of his chest when he'd started undressing had discomposed her even further. He'd looked even broader and more sculpted than he had when she'd been nursing him, his stomach knotted with muscles that looked solid as a tree trunk—strong and powerful—with a line of hair that drew her eye downwards like an arrow towards... A pulse of excitement coursed through her veins at the memory, almost causing her to stumble again. *Enough!* she scolded herself. No matter how impressive or powerful he'd looked, there was no reason for her to *still* be thinking about him, especially when she had far more important things to be doing. She hadn't been to the edge of the forest since the last new moon and if she left it any longer then the people in the village would start to wonder where she was.

She was pleased to feel a new sense of resolve by the time she reached the roundhouse. She'd go to the edge of the forest today, which meant that she needed to prepare herself for being around people again. First she crouched down by the fire pit, trailing her forefingers through the ashes and then across her cheeks to leave two lines of grey powder. Then she collected a few of the twigs left behind from their game the previous evening and wound them into her still-wet hair, twisting the rest into unruly tendrils. Then she sat back on her haunches, trying to put all thoughts of Danr Sigurdsson out of her mind. It wasn't easy. Even apart from his chest, after just a few short days in his company she'd become almost used to talking again. For her own safety, however, she needed to put all of that aside and go back to being inscrutable. That was what the villagers expected of her, which meant that she'd have to guard her eyes and her tongue even more than usual. The slightest sign of emotion could damage her position and make her vulnerable again.

She was busy loading her basket with herbs when Danr arrived back in the clearing, his eyes widening at the sight of her tangled hair and smeared cheeks, though he didn't make any comment, casually draping his linen cloth over the drying cord instead. She didn't speak to or acknowledge him either, concentrating on her basket, though she could feel his eyes on her lowered head and sense the tension in him, too, as if her silence bothered him. From the sound of it, he was pacing up and down the clearing, moving things that didn't need moving, obviously struggling with holding his tongue.

'I'm sorry,' he burst out at last, dropping down on to his haunches in front of her. 'I behaved badly. You've every right to be furious with me for staring. I was caught by surprise, but it won't happen again. From now on, I'll call ahead or whistle to let you know when I'm coming.'

'You mean some kind of warning?' She looked up at him, her lips twitching at the idea.

'Yes.' He knotted his brows together. 'What's so funny?'

'You don't need to give a warning. You were talking to yourself on your way there.'

'Not to myself, to Halvar.' He looked chagrined and then surprised. 'Wait, you mean you *knew* I was there?'

'Of course.' Despite her resolve to be inscrutable, she couldn't stop herself laughing. 'It's never hard to find you anywhere. You hardly ever stop talking except to eat or sleep.'

For a moment he looked as if he might be offended, before he smiled, too. 'My brother Brandt used to threaten to cut my tongue out.'

'Did that ever stop you?'

'No. I used to talk even more to rile him. Then Alarr, my second brother, would offer to help him by holding me down. He actually sat on me once while Brandt got his seax out. They thought scaring me might do the trick, but I'm stubborn.' He shrugged and looked sheepish. 'So my staring didn't offend you?'

She picked up a clump of dried sage and held it to her nose, breathing in the aroma. 'Why would it offend me?'

'Because you were...' he waved a hand vaguely in her direction '...naked.'

'And?'

'And I'm a man and you're a woman.'

She made a dismissive sound before dropping the sage into her basket. 'There's nothing wrong with nakedness. I'm not ashamed of my body.'

'No, but I shouldn't have looked—and I *definitely* shouldn't have stared. It wasn't fitting.'

'Because you're not my mate?'

'Ye-es...' he cleared his throat '... I suppose so.'

'Do you *want* to be my mate?' she asked, tipping her head to one side as the thought suddenly occurred to her. It seemed unlikely, but it would explain the heat she'd seen in his eyes… It was an interesting idea, too, though not one she could ever consider. Her life was solitary for a reason.

'What?'

'Is that why you stared? Because you want to mate with me?'

'I don't… I mean… I wasn't…' His answer, whatever it was, sounded more like a series of coughs than actual words.

She waited a few more moments in case anything more coherent was forthcoming and then stood up, hoisting her basket over her arm. 'I don't know what you just said, but I don't want a mate. I told you, I live alone and you sleep outside.'

'Good. I mean, not good. It's not that I *don't* want to mate with you, but I can't. It's hard to expl—'

'Keep away from the west side of the forest today,' she interrupted him, surprised to feel a combination of relief *and* disappointment at his words. 'There'll be people there.'

'Why? Where are you going?' He pushed himself up off his haunches, his expression shifting to one of concern. 'The village is west of the forest. Surely you're not going there?'

'No.' She whistled for Tove. 'Just close to it. The villagers come to me if they're sick or injured.'

'But I thought you said you didn't want anything to do with people?' His tone turned accusing. 'You said they couldn't be trusted. Why help them?'

'Because Coblaith taught me to be a healer. She gave me a purpose in life so that's what I do. That's why I healed you…' she lifted an eyebrow '…even though you're a warrior. I tend to people and they give me things in exchange.'

'What kinds of things?'

'Milk, eggs, cheese. Things I can't produce for myself.'

'No.' He folded his arms. 'You can't go.'

'It's *my* decision, not yours.' She thrust her jaw out. 'You're only here because I allow it, Norseman, not the other way around.'

'It's too dangerous.'

'Why? I go every moon cycle.'

'Because the man I fought with, Joarr, lives there now. He might suspect that you know something about me. He might ask you questions.'

'I don't speak. The villagers know that.'

'He might still be suspicious.'

'It will look more suspicious if I don't go.'

His brow clenched. 'I still can't let you go alone.'

'You can and you will. No one tells me where I can and can't go.'

'What if you need defending?'

'Then I have this…' she reached for her spear '…and two wolves. I don't need a *warrior* to protect me.' She started away and then looked back over her shoulder, clicking her tongue for Halvar, who immediately sat down.

'Go.' To her irritation, Danr gestured with his hand, urging the big wolf to follow. After a moment's hesitation, he did, sauntering reluctantly across the clearing to join her.

She narrowed her eyes, resenting both his and the wolf's behaviour. 'I'm in charge of my own life and I make my own decisions. *Don't* follow me.'

Chapter Nine

Danr crouched down on his haunches, placing Bitter-blade within easy reach on the ground, before peering out from behind the edge of the boulder. There were several large ones here, scattered all along the edge of the forest, evidence of a rockfall from many years before. Which was particularly convenient since they gave him the opportunity to watch Erika-Bersa—he still hadn't quite decided which name to call her—without her knowledge.

She was standing just beyond the tree line, look-ing out over the sea loch to the hills beyond, Tove on one side, Halvar on the other, as still and silent as a boulder herself. He'd been afraid he might arrive too late, since he'd had to follow at a cautious distance and keep upwind in case the wolves caught his scent, but by the look of things none of the villagers had ar-rived yet. Even so, he was further away from her than he would have liked. What if she needed him? What if Joarr threatened her? What if the massive sea eagle swooping low over the water decided to aim its ferocious-looking beak at her head?

None of which was likely, he knew. He was overreacting about all of it. It would make no sense for Joarr or any of the villagers to threaten or attack her. Never mind that she'd lived in this forest by herself for three years *without* anyone else's protection. She'd only been telling the truth when she'd said she didn't need him, but he still hadn't been able to let her come alone. The thought of her being in potential danger made his heart thump and his chest feel tight—much the way he'd felt when she'd asked if he wanted to mate with her. For the first few seconds after she'd said the words, he'd assumed he must have misheard, or misinterpreted her at least, but she'd definitely said *mate,* as if the idea were actually within the realms of possibility. Of course it hadn't taken her long to add that she didn't *want* a mate—which had come as both a massive relief and a crushing blow at the same time. Even now he wasn't sure which emotion was dominant. It *ought* to be relief, he knew, but if he were completely honest…

Fortunately, at that moment his attention was distracted by the arrival of a small group of people, five in total, two women and three men, one of them leading a horse with a litter trailing behind. As they came closer, he could just make out the shape of a person lying on the back. *Six* people, then, though the last seemed in no condition to fight. They stopped a few feet away from Erika-Bersa, one of the women gesturing towards the litter, and then another man stepped forward and… *Joarr?* Danr was halfway to his feet, clenching the grip of his sword before common sense prevailed. For a fleeting second he thought he saw Erika-Bersa's head twist slightly towards him, before he dropped down behind the boulder and it was impossible to tell.

He took a calming breath and stretched out flat on his stomach, wriggling around the other side of the boulder to watch what was happening. Erika-Bersa was leaning over the litter now while the other villagers had fallen back, waiting with anxious expressions while she performed her ministrations. Only Joarr hadn't moved, standing exactly where he'd been before.

Danr kept his eyes fastened on the old warrior's face, watching for any sign of aggression, but fortunately he seemed calm. When she'd finished tending to the person on the litter, Erika-Bersa stood up and another man approached her, rolling his sleeve up to show her his wrist. She examined it, passed him something from her basket and then one of the women came closer, handing her a bundle which she took without looking at her. Finally, Joarr himself stepped forward, saying a few words before lifting his tunic and pointing at his side.

Danr gritted his teeth, watching in horror as Erika-Bersa reached into her basket again, withdrew a small pot, dipped her fingers inside and then rubbed them over his enemy's torso. His bare torso! Anger shot through him, accompanied by a bolt of jealousy so fierce he could actually see red spots dancing in front of his eyes. It didn't matter that she didn't know who Joarr was. He'd *told* her that the person who'd tried to kill him lived in the village! And if Joarr was showing her a sword wound then surely it wasn't hard to work out that he'd been in a sword fight recently? Couldn't she *guess* who he was? Didn't she have *any* loyalty?

No. The thought brought with it a fresh burst of anger. Of course she didn't have any loyalty to him. She was only tolerating him under sufferance, that was all. He didn't mean anything to her, no more than she ought to mean anything to him. She didn't even want him there! And that made him even angrier.

He waited until she'd finished with Joarr before sliding Bitterblade into his scabbard and storming away.

Sissa didn't look back. It was one of her rules. Looking back suggested either interest or fear and when it came to her dealings with the villagers she was determined to show neither—especially now, in front of the old warrior whose eyes she could feel boring into the space between her shoulder blades.

He'd asked her about Danr, or at least about whether she'd seen an injured warrior with flaxen hair and a cut to his upper arm, and it hadn't been hard to guess the reason. Even if he hadn't also walked with a slight limp, his questions would have given his identity away. This was the man who'd tried to kill Danr, the one he'd called Joarr…

She kept walking, glancing sideways briefly towards a crushed patch of grass beside a boulder on the edge of the clearing. Just as she'd suspected, Danr had followed her, though she wasn't as angry about it as she'd expected to be. Even though he'd gone against her wishes, part of her was actually touched that he'd been worried enough to follow her.

She went deeper into the forest for a while, making sure she wasn't being followed, before heading back to the clearing. The afternoon sky was leaden, threatening heavy rain to come, though Danr appeared to have made no further progress on his shelter. Instead, he was busily chopping logs when she arrived, swinging an axe in his left hand with such force that he looked in danger of splintering the chopping block, too. He'd removed his tunic so that his chest was bare except for the leather pouch he always wore around his neck and his trousers hung low on his hips, giving her an unobscured view of rippling back muscles as he swung back and forth.

She stopped, enthralled by the sight for a few seconds, before realising what she was doing and hurrying inside to put her basket away. Carefully, she hung the leftover herbs up in the rafters of the roundhouse, then put the pots inside a coffer just the way Coblaith had shown her. Then she picked up a comb and went back outside, sitting down by the fire pit as she started to unravel the knots in her hair.

Danr, she noticed, was chopping wood even *more* vigorously than before. It was obvious he was upset, though he could hardly tell her why without also revealing that he'd followed her. Still, she had a feeling he wouldn't be able to remain silent for long—and it was no hardship watching his half-naked body in the meantime. In truth, it was quite engrossing. Surprisingly affecting, too, if the tingling sensation in her abdomen were anything to go by...

She sucked in a breath as muscles flexed in his back and shoulders. Now that the idea of mating had occurred to her, it was proving alarmingly hard to put out of her thoughts again. What was it he'd said that morning? *It's not that I don't want to mate with you...* What did *that* mean? That he actually *wanted* to mate with her? Which begged the question, did *she* want to mate with him? A *warrior*?

She pursed her lips. Taking a mate wasn't a possibility that had ever occurred to her before. She lived on her own because she was safer that way, yet for the first time she was tempted. Something about him set her body to humming in a way she'd never experienced before, a way that she wanted to explore further... But he'd said that he *couldn't* mate. Why not?

'Ow!' The comb snagged on a tangle and she muttered an oath under her breath.

'What?' Danr's head spun round at once.

'Nothing. I wasn't speaking to you.'

'You said something.'

'But not to you.' She gave him a pointed look and tugged harder on the offending knot.

'How was your morning?' His gaze narrowed slightly. 'Any interesting patients?'

'A woman suffering from stomach pains, a man with a burn on his wrist and a warrior with two cracked ribs.'

'And?'

'And I did what I could for them.'

'Is that so?' His gaze sharpened even further. 'So how does it work? Do they tell you their symptoms?'

'No. They gesture. They don't know if I can speak or understand their language.'

'So *they* don't speak either?'

'Not usually.'

'And what about today?'

'What does today matter?'

He flung his axe on to the ground. 'I'd like to know if any of them asked you questions.'

'You tell me.' She finally succeeded in dragging the comb through the knot. 'You were there.'

'So I was.' There was a moment's heavy silence before he spoke again. 'I wanted to be sure you were safe.'

'I told you not to follow me. I let you stay on condition that you obeyed my rules, remember?'

'This seemed more important.'

'That's not the point.'

He clenched his jaw though his expression was unreadable. 'How did you know?'

She considered the question for a moment. How *had* she known? Tove and Halvar hadn't given any indication. She'd thought she'd caught a glimpse of some movement at one point although she hadn't actually seen him, yet somehow she'd simply *known* he was there. She'd been aware of him as surely as if he'd been standing right next to her.

'I saw the grass where you'd been lying,' she said instead. Which was true, even if it had only confirmed what she'd already suspected.

'It could have been crushed by a deer.'

'But it wasn't.'

'No.' His jaw hardened again. 'What did he say, the big man who spoke to you?'

'He asked me if I'd seen an injured warrior.'

'Then you knew who he was!' Danr's eyes flashed accusingly. 'You helped him even though you knew he was the one who did this to me!'

'Yes. I help people who need it.' Calmly, she disentangled a twig from the back of her neck. 'Just because he's your enemy doesn't make him mine.'

'Then you're on *his* side.' Danr folded his arms belligerently.

'I'm on nobody's side. I didn't tell him anything.'

'You still could have—'

'No!' She put the comb down abruptly. 'You can't expect me to take sides when I don't even know what the argument is and you can't expect me not to help someone without telling me why.' She levelled a stare at him. 'You talk about everything else. Why not about why you're here?'

'Because some things aren't easy to talk about!'

'Do you think *I* don't know that?'

'You're right.' He looked around the clearing and rubbed a hand over his face. '*Of course* you know that, but it's not as if you've told me much either. All I know is that you speak Norse and that you learnt healing from a Gael woman who rescued you from the forest. I have no idea who you are or where you came from. I don't even know your name.'

'And all *I* know is that you came here for answers from a man with two cracked ribs and that you never say two words when ten will do! I don't owe you an explanation. That was part of our agreement. You're the one who came and asked for my help!'

They glared at each other for a few seconds, their jaws clenched, before he sighed and sat down on the tree stump. 'Joarr was my father's helmsman and my friend. My *good* friend. He was like a father to me once.'

She lifted her chin. 'He came to the island with a woman over a year ago. I've seen him a few times, but he's never asked for my help before.'

'Will his ribs heal?'

'Yes. As long as he doesn't get into any more fights.'

'I never wanted to fight him in the first place. He's a kinsman of Knut's, but he's not the one I need to speak to. I came to Skíð for the woman—Hilda. She's my father's widow, my stepmother of sorts, although she hates to be called that. She's married to Joarr now.'

'So you came to ask questions of her?'

'Yes.' He lowered his head, his shoulders heaving as if at some heavy burden hanging around them. 'I came to find out if she murdered my father.'

Chapter Ten

Danr laid his forearms across his knees, staring at the ground beneath his feet. It was mostly compact earth with a scattering of twigs and pine needles, as well as five woodlice, one spider and a pair of ants skittering towards the stump. Erika-Bersa hadn't made any response to his last statement, presumably because she was waiting for him to explain, but it was hard to know where to begin. With the massacre on Alarr's wedding day? No, if he was going to tell her about Hilda then he had to go back even further, back to the aftermath of his mother's death.

'I told you that Rurik and I moved into our father's hall after our mother died. He was the Jarl, but we were acknowledged as his bastards. I looked so much like him that it would have been hard for him *not* to acknowledge us, but we were still treated differently from his other sons. Hilda saw to that.'

'You mentioned Brandt and Alarr before.'

'Yes. Brandt is the eldest, Alarr was born the same

summer as Rurik and I, then Sandulf is the youngest. We were always close, as close as full brothers could be, but Hilda hated Rurik and me from the start. She let us know that she didn't want us there and in return I made it clear I loathed her, too. I thought it was the least I could do for my mother.'

'Didn't your father intervene? Try to make peace?'

He gave a curt laugh. 'Peace was never high on the list of my father's priorities. Our feud amused him. And I was just a bastard, after all. It didn't really matter how I behaved or what I said. He liked me to be wild. He liked to hear of my exploits, too. Stupid, dangerous things at first, like diving from cliffs into the sea or fighting other boys twice my size, but as I grew older, it became all about women.' He looked up to watch her reaction. 'For some reason women always liked me. It was almost *too* easy to bed them. And the more women I bedded, the more it amused my father. Sometimes he invited me on to the high bench at *nattmal* just so I could tell him about my latest partner. He always made sure it was in Hilda's hearing, too.'

'Do you mean mates?' She drew her brows together, her expression faintly quizzical.

'*Temporary* mates, yes. They were all willing, but some of them wanted more from me than I could give. Marriage, commitment...' He dropped his gaze back to the dirt. 'I treated them badly. All I thought about was myself, never their feelings.'

'So you treated them the way your father treated your mother?'

'What?' He jerked his head up again, angry at the

comparison. 'No! I never deceived a woman the way he did my mother. I never laid hands on an innocent either. All those women knew what they wanted. Half of them only wanted to bed the Jarl's son.'

'You just admitted that you never considered their feelings. It sounds similar to me.'

'Well, it wasn't. I might have let them deceive themselves, but I never promised them anything.' He winced and muttered an oath. 'Which maybe isn't much better. Perhaps I'm even more like my father than I realised. Hilda said I was empty and shallow, that I had inherited the very worst of his qualities.'

'Maybe that's the reason she disliked you.'

'Are you siding with *her* now, too?' He glowered across the fire pit. 'But the fact that she hated my behaviour only spurred me on. There was no love lost between her and my father by that point, but they both seemed to have the best interests of Maerr at heart. Then, about three years ago, I noticed her acting differently. Joarr, too. I knew enough about conducting secret affairs to guess what was happening.'

'Did you tell your father?'

'That he was a cuckold? No.'

'Why not? Especially if you disliked her so much?'

'I'm not sure. Maybe because I didn't entirely blame her for betraying my father. Maybe because I didn't want him to kill Joarr in retaliation. I knew that if it carried on then he'd find out sooner or later, but I'd hoped Joarr would come to his senses before then.'

'But he didn't?'

'No. Then a little while afterwards, my father arranged my brother Alarr's betrothal. It was a good match, one that would have made Maerr more powerful than ever. Guests came from all over for the wedding and there was going to be a great feast, followed by days of celebration. Then a few hours before the ceremony was about to begin, a messenger came with news of trouble to the north. Brandt and Rurik went to deal with it, leaving me and Sandulf behind.' He stood up, too agitated to keep still now that the words were flowing. 'It seemed a much better alternative at the time, even though there was a strange atmosphere in the air, too. I couldn't place my finger on what it was exactly, but it was a kind of tension, as if people were waiting for something to happen. I put it down to the excitement of the wedding.' He realised that he'd paced to the far side of the clearing and turned around again. 'The ceremony had barely started before the assassins struck. Our father didn't stand a chance. Alarr was badly injured and his betrothed Gilla and Brandt's wife Ingrid were slain in cold blood. Ingrid was carrying a babe at the time.'

He stopped pacing to look at her. Her skin had turned a deathly shade of pale and her expression was even more horrified than he'd expected. For a moment he wondered whether he should have told her his story after all.

'Go on.' Even her voice sounded different, as if she were forcing the words through clenched teeth.

'It was a massacre. They burnt half our boats and houses. By the end, almost our whole village was destroyed.'

'I'm sorry.' The words were oddly clipped. 'But what about you? Were you injured as well?'

'No.' He flinched even though he'd been waiting for the question. 'When the attack started I was...elsewhere.'

'You mean you were lured away like your brothers?'

'Something like that.' He felt bile rise in his throat. Perhaps he ought to tell her the whole truth, but just the thought of it made him feel sick. 'By the time I realised what was happening it was too late to save my family. I helped to put out fires and did what I could, but...' He curled his hands into fists. 'It wasn't enough, not even close to enough. I should have been there.'

'Do you think you could have stopped what happened?'

'No.' He shook his head. 'There were too many of them and they were too well organised, but the assassins must have come for my father, not Ingrid or Gilla. Maybe I could have saved them. I would have given my life if it could have saved either of them.'

She was silent for a few moments. 'And you really think your stepmother was behind it?'

'I think she's involved somehow, though I admit it took me a while to see it. She seemed as distraught as anyone to begin with. It never occurred to any of us to suspect her.' He sat down on the stump again. 'But we've been following clues, my brothers and I. Alarr and Rurik went to Eireann, Brandt and I pursued leads in Alba, and Sandulf travelled all the way to Constantinople where he came upon some of the assassins. Gradually the clues all pointed towards Hilda. That's why I've come here, to discover the truth once and for all.' He sighed regretfully. 'I just wasn't very tactful about it.'

'You mean you just asked her outright?' Her brow furrowed again. 'That doesn't sound like a very good plan, especially if she's as ruthless as she sounds.'

'It wasn't.'

'And why were you the one sent to confront her? If she hates you so much, wouldn't it have been safer for one of her own sons to do it?'

'Probably, but Rurik and I are the only ones she can't manipulate. Besides, there wasn't much choice. Sandulf discovered the evidence that implicated her, but he had to go to Eireann. I'm supposed to join him and our other brothers there before winter to tell them what I discover.' He made a wry face. 'I'm usually the best at making plans.'

'You?'

'I said usually, not always.' He scowled as her gaze flickered to his arm. 'You don't have to look so surprised. I had a lapse in judgement, but in my defence, I intended to go to the village first, to pretend that I was just passing through and then speak to Joarr before I confronted Hilda. Only when I arrived she was all alone and it seemed too good an opportunity to miss. My temper got the better of me. When Joarr found us I was pointing my sword at her throat.' He spread his hands out. 'You can see why he was angry.'

'Don't you think he might have been involved, too? If he could betray your father's trust with his wife, then maybe he might have betrayed him in other ways?'

'No.' Danr shook his head adamantly. 'I saw Joarr fighting on our side that day. He would never have murdered our people. Unfortunately, he's blind when it comes to Hilda. No doubt she's lied to him and he believes her.' He sighed. 'So that's my story, the reason I'm here.'

'Mmm.'

'That's all you have to say?' He lifted an eyebrow in surprise. Considering what he'd just told her it seemed a somewhat lukewarm response… No words of sympathy or condolence, just *mmm,* almost as if she doubted the truth of his words. 'What do you mean, "mmm"?'

'I'm not sure yet. I'm thinking.'

'What is there to think about?'

'Shhh.' She waved a hand to quiet him, staring with pursed lips and a look of intense concentration into the distance for a while before shaking her head. 'No. It doesn't make sense.'

'What? Which part?'

'The part about your stepmother being responsible. Did she hate your brothers' women, the ones who died?'

'No. She was fond of them both, especially Ingrid.'

'Then why would she have killed them? Her own grandchild, too?'

'I doubt that was supposed to happen. Things probably got out of control. Maybe that's why she was so upset afterwards.'

'But you said that your brother Alarr was badly injured as well. Why would she have ordered an attack on her own son's wedding? Surely there were other occasions she could have used? Why risk him and your other brother, Sandulf?'

'I just told you, because things got out of hand.'

'No.' Her tone was infuriatingly matter of fact. 'If all she'd wanted was to leave her husband then there are easier ways. Why so much violence?'

'It's not just a theory. I have proof!' He reached for the leather pouch he kept on a cord around his neck, tipping the contents into his hand. 'These are the pendants Rurik and Sandulf discovered were used to pay the assassins. They recognised them as ones that belonged to Hilda, presents our father gave her after the birth of each of their sons.'

'They look valuable.' She reached a hand out, running a finger over one of the gold and silver ridged arrows. 'Still…'

'What now?'

'That's evidence, not proof. Did the assassins *say* she was involved?'

'No. We never gave them a chance.'

'We?'

'Sandulf killed one in Constantinople. I killed another in Strathclyde.' He frowned, feeling a need to defend his actions. 'The man was a cold-blooded monster *and* he was about to kill Sandulf.'

'Then what about Hilda? What did she say when you asked her about them? Did *she* have an explanation?'

'I don't know.' He cleared his throat awkwardly. 'I didn't get that far. Joarr found us before I could even mention the pendants.'

'So you didn't think to ask her about them *before* you threatened her at swordpoint?'

'As I said, I lost my temper, but it was a bluff. I thought I could make her confess.'

She rolled her eyes. 'What do you think your brothers would say if you told them this?'

He gave a brusque laugh. 'Brandt wouldn't say anything. He'd just glower. Alarr would call me a fool. Rurik would give me a shove and then try to defend me and Sandulf would probably shake his head and say it was all his fault somehow.'

'Well, at least you know you acted stupidly.'

'You know you can stop talking again whenever you want.' He clenched his jaw. 'Yes, I acted stupidly, but that doesn't mean I'm wrong about Hilda.'

'It doesn't prove that you're right, either.' She leaned forward towards him. 'Using her own jewellery to pay the assassins doesn't make any sense. Why would she use anything that could be traced back to her so easily?'

'Because she never thought she'd be found out.'

'But she would have known that her sons would want revenge for their father. That means she would have known there was a strong chance they'd go after the assassins. Why would she have risked them recognising these pendants?'

'Maybe she made a mistake.'

'The kind of person who could plan such an intricate attack doesn't sound like someone who makes mistakes. A clever person would have used gold.'

'Then maybe she's not as clever as she thinks.'

'Or maybe you just want her to be guilty?'

Danr stiffened at the accusation. *Was* that what he wanted? Looking back, he knew he'd wanted to accuse Hilda. That was why he'd rushed in to confront her when he should have waited. He'd *wanted* to hear her confess. He still did, but was it possible that she was innocent? Maybe Erika-Bersa was right and he'd let hatred prejudice his judgement.

'Why are you defending her?' He sought refuge in anger. 'Even if she's not guilty of this, she's guilty of other things—of the way she treated Rurik and me! Of betraying my father with his own helmsman!'

'Yes.' She seemed nonplussed by his reaction. 'But that's not why you're here.'

The words, spoken so softly, seemed to defuse his anger. 'You're right, but I *need* to find out the truth. I need to find out who murdered my family and get justice for them.'

'I know. That's why you should take a branch of peace and go and speak to your stepmother properly. It's what you ought to have done in the first place.'

'Something tells me a branch of peace isn't going to stop Joarr from killing me now.'

'Mmm, perhaps not.' She pressed her lips together thoughtfully. 'But there has to be a peaceful way.'

'Let me know if you think of one.'

'I will.' There was a long moment of silence before she spoke again, her voice wavering slightly. 'Danr, I'm sorry about your father and your womenfolk. It must have been a terrible thing to witness. I know how it feels to lose people you care about.'

'You mean your family?' He held on to her gaze, almost afraid to breathe unless it disturbed the new atmosphere of confidence between them. 'Is that why you're alone? Will you tell me what happened to them?'

She seemed to hesitate before glancing up at the sky and shaking her head. 'Not now. I'm tired and there's more rain coming. Heavy rain this time.' She stood up and hesitated again. 'Sissa. That's my name. And I was born here on the island.'

'Sissa…' His heart warmed suddenly. 'Thank you.'

'Now, you should fix the roof of your shelter. It has holes.'

Chapter Eleven

A drop of water splashed on to Danr's cheek. He rolled on to his good side to avoid it and put his face in a patch of soggy and foul-tasting moss instead. He muttered an oath and rolled back again, listening to the sound of rain outside. Although he noticed it wasn't just one sound. It was several. Quick splashes, slow splashes, soft splashes, heavy splashes—none of which sounded as if they had any intention of stopping any time soon. His pelt roof had obviously blown away and now an icy wind was finding its way through every nook and cranny in his shelter, of which there appeared to be many, chilling all the wet patches of his clothing. He'd lain down less than an hour ago and now he had a sinking feeling that it was going to be a very long night.

He gave up trying to sleep, propping himself up on his elbows to look outside. Despite the rain, the moon was still bright enough for him to make out the shape of the roundhouse in the centre of the clearing. There was a trail of smoke twisting up from the hole in the roof, unlike his own fire, which had long since given up its battle with the elements. Not surprisingly, Halvar had already abandoned him. He really *should* have devoted more time and attention to building his shelter, Danr thought regretfully. He probably ought to do something about it now, though how exactly he was going to block up so many holes in the dark he had no idea. Maybe if he asked nicely, Sissa would let him spend the night in her cave. It would be freezing, but at least he'd be dry.

Sissa. Just the thought of her warmed him a little. He felt pleased and honoured that she'd finally trusted him enough to tell him her name. Now that he knew it, it seemed so obvious, too. How could he ever have thought her a Bersa? She couldn't be anything but Sissa. It suited her. Just like her wild hair and oyster-pearl eyes suited her... They were what made her beautiful. Or at least beautiful in her own way. A way that he was finding more and more appealing. Not that sitting there thinking about that was going to do anything to keep him dry. If he wasn't careful he'd catch a fever...

He crawled forward and heaved himself to his feet, ready to make a valiant and probably pointless attempt to repair his shelter, when the leather curtain of the roundhouse moved aside and Sissa's narrow face peered out.

'Are you awake?' She spoke in a loud whisper.

'Very!'

'Then come here!'

'What?' For a moment he wondered if he'd fallen asleep after all and was dreaming.

'Come here unless you want to catch your death, but hurry up.' She lifted a hand to beckon him. 'The heat's escaping.'

He didn't wait to be told again, jumping to his feet and hurrying across the clearing, ducking his head under the doorway to step inside. The space within was illuminated by firelight and looked far bigger than he'd expected, with a raised central hearth framed by a bench on one side, an old wooden coffer on the other and a pile of furs opposite the door, above which hung an assortment of herbs that gave the air a pungent, almost heady aroma. Tove and Halvar were already asleep, he noticed, stretched out on the floor with their heads pressed together and snoring softly. It all looked snug and cosy and inviting. *Too* snug and cosy and inviting, it struck him suddenly. Three years ago, he would have been more than happy to be trapped in such a place with a woman. Now he wondered if the frigid cave might have been a wiser idea, after all...

'How have you survived so long, Danr Sigurdsson?' Sissa put her hands on her hips, looking him up and down critically. 'Tomorrow we'll build you a better shelter, but right now you should sit by the fire for a while. You'll dry soon enough.'

'Thank you.' He ruffled his hands through his hair and sat down on the bench. 'I never did like rain.'

'I know. It was one of the first things you said to me.'

'You remember that?' He felt absurdly pleased by the fact. 'I didn't think you were listening to me that day.'

'I was. You said you hated drizzle and clouds that hang in the air for days.'

'Doesn't everyone?'

She shrugged. 'The rain feeds the forest. Without the grey days, the bright ones wouldn't be so beautiful.'

'I'd still rather have one big storm than a week of grey.'

'Big storms cause damage. Trees are blown down and animals are frightened. You need more patience, Norseman.' She gave him a chiding look and then clambered on to the pile of furs, pulling her knees to her chest and then tilting her head at the sound of a low rumble of thunder in the distance. 'But perhaps you'll get your wish.'

'Mmm?' Danr lifted his gaze quickly from where her tunic had ridden up to her calves. 'What wish?'

'It sounds as if there's a storm coming.'

'Ah.' He averted his face to stare intently into the fire. It hadn't exactly been what he'd been wishing for at that moment, but as long as she didn't guess what had really been on his mind—or, more specifically, which part of her body... He gritted his teeth, re-ordering his thoughts before glancing back over his shoulder. 'I thought you'd be asleep by now. You said you were tired.'

'I am.' She looked pensive. 'But I was thinking.'

'About my stupidity again?' He quirked an eyebrow, but her expression remained serious.

'About everything you told me. You might have rushed in too quickly by confronting your stepmother, but it was understandable. You thought you'd found the person responsible for destroying your family. Most people would probably have acted the same way. Maybe reckless is a better word.'

'It sounds better.' He smiled wryly. 'Thank you.'

She nodded her head and patted the space next to her on the furs. 'You can sleep here when you're dry.'

'You mean beside you?' He felt as if all the air in the room had just been sucked up through the chimney.

'Yes. You can't sleep on the bench and it's not good to sleep so close to the fire.'

'I can sleep on the floor.'

She gave him a questioning look and then shrugged as if she didn't care either way, wriggling down beneath her furs. 'Do as you please. Only, if you do decide to sleep here don't wake me.'

Sissa opened her eyes, brought back to consciousness by the tumult of wind and rain outside. The rumble of thunder had apparently been just the beginning of a storm. The rain was coming down in torrents now, lashing the sides of the roundhouse, finding its way down the chimney and making the hearth sizzle. She'd found it hard enough getting to sleep at all, firstly because she'd been worried about him freezing to death outside and then, after she'd invited him in, because her mind had still kept on whirling with everything he'd told her. She'd stared at the turf wall beside her head for a long time, thinking. His story had been difficult to listen to, so close to her own that she'd felt her stomach churn and a cold sweat break out on her brow several times. At one point she'd almost begged him to stop, feeling as if she were about to be sick.

Fortunately, she hadn't, mumbling a few brief words of sympathy instead before shifting his attention on to the subject of his stepmother. It had been easier to think about who might have been responsible for the massacre than the events themselves. She didn't blame Danr for suspecting Hilda, but she couldn't help but feel there were holes in his theory. There were other holes in what he'd told her, too, about where he'd been when the massacre had happened, for example, but it was obvious he hadn't wanted to tell her, which meant that, wherever he had been, he felt guilty about it.

She rolled on to her other side and almost bumped into him. She'd assumed that he'd chosen to sleep on the floor since she hadn't felt him get into bed before she'd finally drifted off to sleep, which made his presence beside her something of a surprise now, albeit not an unpleasant one. He was lying on his back, his broad chest rising and falling in a steady rhythm of long, drawn-out breaths. She wasn't sure why she'd invited him into her bed when she might have simply have offered him a fur for the floor, but it had seemed a reasonable idea at the time. Sharing a warm bed on a cold, stormy night was only practical, just as it had been when she'd been nursing him, although she had to admit that her feelings towards him had changed significantly in the few days since. She *still* had no intention of letting him stay any longer than was necessary, but now that she knew his story, he seemed more real somehow, less of a warrior and more of a man. It made it impossible to see him as just a warm body, either. Ever since that moment when their fingers had tangled, she'd found herself becoming more and more curious about him, not to mention more and more tempted to touch him again. It was strange how the idea of touching someone, of *being* touched as well, didn't alarm her in the way it had even a day ago. Now she was aware of a strange yearning sensation, wondering what it would be like to feel his skin against hers. The warmth radiating from his body tempted her to move closer and find out, to reach out and stroke her fingers across his chest, just to see how it felt…

She resisted the impulse, rolling away from him to stare at the ceiling instead.

'Can't you sleep?'

'Oh!' The sound of his voice in her ear made her start guiltily. Had he *known* she'd just been staring at him? 'No. I was thinking again.'

'So was I.' He smiled as she twisted her face back towards him. 'About how glad I am you took pity on me tonight. I would have been washed away by now otherwise.'

'Probably.'

He folded his good arm behind his head, his expression turning serious. 'If you're still thinking about what I told you earlier, then I'm sorry. I didn't mean to upset you.'

'No.' She swallowed, intensely aware of the curve of his bicep beside her. 'I wasn't thinking of that…' Her voice trailed away as heat flared in her chest. How could she tell him what she'd *really* just been thinking? He'd said that he couldn't mate and she didn't even know if she wanted to, but on the other hand, why *not* talk to him about it? He was the one who liked talking so much. What was the worst that could happen? He could walk out and leave? She'd already told him to do that. Repeatedly.

'You.' She spoke before she could change her mind. 'I was thinking about you.'

'Me?' She saw a flash of something in his eyes, quickly extinguished. 'Then I'm flattered.'

'Why can't you mate?'

'Why...?' This time his expression seemed to freeze. 'What?'

'When I asked if you wanted to mate with me, you said you couldn't. Why not?'

'It's complicated.' He gave a small cough. 'And you said you didn't want a mate.'

'I don't, but I'm still curious.' She ran her tongue over her bottom lip as her mouth turned dry. 'Do you already have a mate?'

'You mean a wife?' He shifted beneath the furs, re-arranging them slightly on top of him. 'No.'

'But you said that women liked you?'

'They always seemed to, yes.'

'So you like mating, but not having a mate?'

'Ye-es, I suppose so. I *did* anyway.'

'Some people come into the forest to mate.' She drew her brows together. 'It looks strange. Not the way animals do it.'

'Really?' There was a pained, slightly husky note to his voice all of a sudden.

'They look at each other, with their faces together, like this.' She leaned towards him at the same moment as there was a loud crack of thunder above. 'But they seem to enjoy it.'

'Yes, it can be…pleasurable either way.'

'You mean there's more than one way for people?'

'A few…'

'A *few*?' Both her eyebrows shot up in surprise. 'What are the others?'

'This may not be the best time to discuss it.' He cleared his throat, not that it seemed to help. His voice sounded even huskier, as if he were having trouble getting words out at all.

'Are you all right? Here.' She sat up and leaned over him, reaching for the flagon of water she kept beside the bed. 'Drink some of this.'

'Sissa…' He sounded as if he were in some kind of pain.

'What? You sound like you need it.'

'I need something.'

She gave him a puzzled look and lay down again, one hand resting beneath her cheek. 'So what does it feel like?'

'What?' He paused with the flagon against his lips.

'Mating? *How* is it pleasurable?'

'I don't know. It's hard to describe.'

'*You're* at a loss for words?'

'Some words, yes.' He took a long swallow and put the flagon aside. 'Particularly those ones.'

'You won't even *try* to describe it?'

'Moon's eye, woman.' He spun his face towards her again. 'I'm trying to be good!'

'But you just said that mating was pleasurable!'

'It is. *Very* pleasurable sometimes, but I'm trying to be good with *you*. You're an innocent.'

'But *I* asked.'

He muttered something under his breath. 'All right. It's like losing yourself. You don't think, you just feel.'

'Mmm.' She rolled on to her back again, feeling even more curious. Could *mating* really be as pleasurable as he said? Would it be pleasurable with him?

It wasn't until he inhaled sharply that she realised she'd just asked the question aloud. Heat flooded her body, but now that she'd asked…

'Would I find it pleasurable with you?' she repeated the question. 'If you and I were to mate, I mean.'

'Sissa!' He let out something between a cough and an expletive. 'Trust me, I'm not good mate material.'

'I'm only asking *what if*. I'm curious.'

'Curiosity can be dangerous.'

'But I want to know…'

Chapter Twelve

Sissa felt the hairs on the backs of her arms and neck prickle.

Curiosity can be dangerous…

That was definitely true. Until Danr had arrived, her life had been one of silence and safety. Somehow he'd made it more dangerous and yet she couldn't bring herself to turn away from him either. Instead, she felt as though every nerve in her body was humming, waiting for something to happen. She could sense a similar tension in him, too. Just his expression made her feel breathless. He reminded her of Halvar when he was stalking his prey, crouching low, taking his time, waiting for the perfect moment…

She ran the tip of her tongue over her bottom lip, repeating her question a third time. 'I want to know… would it be pleasurable with you?'

'There would be some pain at first, but I would make it pleasurable.' His eyes looked hooded. 'I could make it pleasurable for you.'

'You mean those things you said when you first came here? The ones that made me angry?'

'Yes.' One of his hands moved to skim the side of her hip. 'If that's what you really want?'

'I didn't say that.' She was the one to clear her throat this time. Her breath was coming in shorter, almost ragged bursts, making it hard to think clearly. The situation seemed even more dangerous now and yet she wasn't afraid of him either. Somehow she knew he wouldn't hurt her or do anything she didn't want. It was *herself* she was afraid of. If only she knew *what* it was she wanted… 'But *if* we did…how would we start?'

'Well…' His hand trailed upwards, stroking across her stomach. 'We'd probably start with a kiss.'

'Like this?' She wriggled closer, pressing her lips lightly against his. It was the way Birger had once kissed her on the cheek.

'Ye-es.' His eyes glowed brighter in the firelight, like stars in the darkness. 'Only, perhaps more like this…'

Before she could ask what he intended, his mouth had found hers again, touching softly at first as if he were encouraging her to trust him, then with a harder pressure accompanied by a strangled sound from the back of his throat. His lips were warm and firm and seemed to have some kind of destabilising effect on the rest of her body, flooding her limbs with warmth and making her inner organs perform a series of strange and startling contortions. Her heart seemed to have leapt into her throat and her stomach was busy twisting itself into some kind of knot. It all felt alarming and exciting at the same time, as if the thunder and lightning outside had somehow burst into the roundhouse with them, eclipsing thought and leaving only a building fervour behind. After a momentary hesitation, she let herself yield to the feeling, embracing and savouring every reaction even when his tongue slid along the seam of her lips, coaxing them apart and then dipping past them into her mouth.

'Danr?' She murmured his name as they came apart finally.

'Mmm?' His lips drifted to the curve of her throat, nuzzling beneath her chin while one of his hands slid around to the small of her back, drawing her even closer towards him.

'What would come next?' She sounded as if she were panting.

'Next I would kiss you here.' He moved his head lower, dragging the neck of her shift down over one shoulder and trailing his lips along the line of her collarbone, then darting his tongue out to kiss the hollow at the base of her neck. 'And here...and all over...'

'And what would *I* do?'

'Whatever you wanted.' His lips stilled for a moment. 'You could kiss me, too, or touch me, or just lie back and enjoy it.'

She decided to try all three suggestions at once, closing her eyes as she smoothed her hands over his shoulders and back, tracing the contours of each corded muscle. Surges of pleasure pulsed in small waves through her body and the knot in her stomach tightened almost painfully. Except that it wasn't quite her stomach. It was lower than that, between her thighs, thighs and hips that had started to move and strain upwards of their own accord. It seemed almost impossible to keep still.

'Sissa.' He growled her name and she tipped her head back, seized with a new thrill of excitement. His body was straining against hers in a way that left her in no doubt about what he wanted and how much he wanted it. She wanted it, too, she realised, and just as badly. She was a long way beyond curiosity now and in more danger than she'd imagined was possible when she'd simply asked how it would feel, yet she still couldn't bring herself to stop. Instead, she trailed her hands across his chest, amazed at how hard and solid he felt beneath her fingertips, sliding them around his neck and into his hair as his lips claimed hers again. She felt... What did she feel? As if she were trying to reach some elusive peak of feeling, but also that she never wanted it to end...

They moaned simultaneously as one of his legs slid between her thighs, nudging them gently but firmly apart. And then a hand gripped the hem of her shift, drawing it up around her waist, and she felt a flutter of panic. Touching and kissing him was one thing, but this was too much, too quickly... Something about it didn't feel right. Something was missing. Anxiety overtook excitement. Maybe inviting him into her bed had been a mistake, after all. Even aside from the sheer *overwhelmingness* of it, there could be other consequences, too, ones that she wasn't ready to deal with... She opened her mouth, about to protest, when he moved away suddenly, muttering an oath as he rolled to the other side of the bed.

'Danr?' She sat up, her body still tingling from his touch, her emotions torn between relief and surprise as she pulled her shift back up around her shoulders.

'I'm sorry.' He half-turned his head though he didn't look at her, his voice thick-sounding. 'I can't. I want to, but I can't. And curiosity isn't a good enough reason, trust me. It...*mating,* should mean more.'

'You mean love?'

He looked briefly over his shoulder and then away again. 'Yes.'

'Oh.' She looked down at her hands. Just a moment ago they'd been pressed against his skin, caressing, exploring, taking pleasure from the heat and silken feel of his body. Now they felt cold and empty, but curiosity wasn't enough... She pursed her lips. He was right. It was the conclusion she'd just come to as well, the reason she'd been about to ask him to stop. She only wished that she'd been the one to say it first.

If only she hadn't invited him into the roundhouse! *If only* the storm hadn't awoken her! *If only* he'd told her that curiosity wasn't enough beforehand! But he *had*, she realised. He'd been trying to deter her from the start, telling her he was trying to be good and saying he wasn't 'mate material'. Her cheeks flamed as an even worse thought occurred to her. What if she'd been mistaken about him desiring her *at all*? What if he'd only gone along with things because he'd felt he *had* to? Because she might not have let him stay otherwise...

'I'm sorry.' He was speaking again, she realised with a jolt. 'I shouldn't have kissed you in the first place.'

'You didn't.' Her voice sounded hoarse. 'I kissed you first because I was curious. It was foolish of me.'

'No. It wasn't foolish, it was…' He shook his head, as if he were at a loss for words again. 'But you deserve a real mate, someone to love and cherish you. I'm not that man. I'm not good or worthy enough and…' his expression looked torn '…even if I were, I made an oath.'

'An oath?' She stared at him, uncomprehending. 'What kind of oath?'

Danr cleared his throat once, twice and then a third time for good measure, not that doing so brought him any kind of relief. His oath wasn't something he wanted to talk about, especially under the present circumstances. He was already alarmed by how close he'd come to breaking it. Even now, with Sissa looking so gut-wrenchingly desirable, all mussed-up hair and kiss-swollen lips, he had to concentrate all his attention on staring at his hands and regulating his breathing just to control the urge to pounce on her again. She'd been *curious* about mating and he'd been severely tempted to assuage that curiosity. He'd wanted to assuage other things, too, but he'd managed to stop himself just in time—although he had an underlying feeling that she'd been about to stop him, too. Something about her body language had changed when he'd drawn her shift up, enough to give him the jolt he'd needed to break their embrace. But he should never have given in to the temptation to touch her in the first place! Which meant that any painful effects he was suffering now were only what he deserved.

'Danr?' Her voice was still slightly breathless, he noticed, enough to send a fresh shiver of desire coursing through his veins. But she'd asked him a question…

'Three years ago I made an oath. Not to…to *mate* until I made some kind of amends for what happened at Alarr's wedding.'

'Oh.' There was a brief pause. 'That sounds like a strange kind of oath.'

'It seemed like the only thing I could do at the time. I had reasons. *One* particular reason.' He sucked in a deep breath and then blew it out slowly between his teeth. 'I *wish* I could mate with you, truly, but I can't.'

'Really?'

'Yes.' He risked another brief look over his shoulder, then wished he hadn't. 'You've no idea how desirable you are, Sissa.'

She made a dismissive sound. 'No, I'm not. I look like a tree.'

'A beautiful tree.' He gave a curt laugh. 'Maybe that's why you belong in the forest.'

'You don't have to say that.'

'Why would I lie?'

'So that I'll let you stay?'

'Is that what you think?' At that precise moment, the idea struck him as several stages beyond ludicrous. 'That I was just *pretending* to desire you?'

'If you were, then it was my fault.' She gave a stiff-looking shrug. 'I shouldn't have asked questions. We should forget it ever happened.'

'Not until we get one thing straight.' He steeled himself and then twisted around, lifting a hand to the side of her face. 'For a start, I'm not that good at pretending. Trust me, it doesn't work that way. For another thing, you're beautiful, Sissa, inside and out. You're strong and brave and… I like your company. I like *you*. You're the first woman in three years I've been even remotely tempted to share a bed with, but I can't.'

'Oh.' She looked faintly stunned.

'I shouldn't have let it go so far. I'm sorry.' He pushed a lock of hair back behind one of her ears, distracted by the ridge of her cheekbone and the dip beneath it. Her skin was soft and smooth, tempting him to place his lips there, but if he did that, then he knew he wouldn't want to stop. He'd want to claim more kisses, in other places. On her chin, her jaw, her eyelids, against the thud of her pulse at the base of her throat…

He was *supposed* to be apologising.

'Don't be sorry.' Her expression softened beneath his touch. 'I started it, but I wanted to stop, too. It wasn't what I expected.'

'You mean you didn't like it?' He snapped his brows together.

'No, it wasn't that. It was just…*more* than I expected. Too much.'

To his own surprise, he found himself leaning forward, pressing his forehead lightly against hers. 'Thank you.'

'For what?'

'For telling me that. It helps. The last thing I'd want is for you to regret anything.'

'So we can forget it ever happened?' She looked relieved when he nodded. 'Good. But I still don't understand. *Why* did you make such an oath?'

'Because it was the least of what I deserved.' He moved back, though he didn't turn away again. If he were going to tell her the truth then he deserved to see her expression, too. He deserved to witness the moment when she realised how unworthy he really was... 'I've been with a lot of women, Sissa. Too many women. I've behaved badly, without thinking about the consequences. It was a weakness my family's enemies were able to use against me.'

'What do you mean?'

'On the day of the wedding, after Rurik and Brandt had ridden north, Alarr and Sandulf were persuaded to leave their weapons outside the wedding hall. With me, however, the assassins knew there was no need for anything so subtle. They knew exactly which weakness to exploit.' He shook his head in self-disgust. 'I was lured to the far side of the village by a woman. She kept me...*distracted* while my kin were slaughtered in cold blood.'

'Distracted?'

He nodded grimly. 'I didn't even hear the fighting until it was almost over.'

'Oh.' She was silent for a long moment. 'And you didn't think it strange that a woman would seduce you just before your brother's wedding?'

'No.' He winced at how incriminating it sounded,

still holding on to her gaze, though the intensity in hers made him feel even worse. What was she thinking? He could feel his chest constricting as he waited for her to pass judgement, though none seemed to be forthcoming.

'Don't you have anything to say?' he asked when he couldn't bear the silence any longer. 'Say what you think. Do your worst. I deserve all your condemnation.'

'You already know everything I might say.'

'Maybe I still want to hear it.'

'I'm not going to condemn you, Danr.'

'Why not?'

'Because what good would it do? You already have to live with what you did. Even aside from your oath, that sounds like punishment enough.'

'It still doesn't feel like enough.'

'No, I suppose not.' She looked thoughtful. 'Were there any signs of trouble at the wedding beforehand?'

He shook his head. 'There were too many people, too many unknown guests who came for the wedding, but the only threat seemed to come from the war band Brandt and Rurik went after.'

'Had you been *told* to stay and guard your family?'

'No, but I still should have been there.' He scowled. 'If you're trying to make excuses for me, then I don't want to hear them.'

'I'm not making excuses, I'm just trying to understand. What happened to the woman afterwards?'

'I've no idea where she went, but I hope I never set eyes on her again. By the time I realised she must have been working for the assassins, she was long gone.

Then all I could do was watch Brandt clutch his dead wife in his arms and think that I could have prevented it. He looked broken, like a man in torment.'

'If you'd tried to prevent it, then you might have been killed, too.'

'At least that would have been honourable.'

'Is that what your brothers said?'

'No.' He clenched his jaw. 'But I wish they had. I wish they'd all been furious with me. I wish Brandt had pummelled my head into the dirt. It might have made me feel a little better, but it was as though they never expected any better from me...' He passed a hand over his face. 'I failed my family because I was an attention-seeking, irresponsible fool, the joker who was always driven by his lust instead of his head, but those days are over. I'm not that man any more. I want to be a better man, a man of worth, someone whose reflection I can bear to look at. That means making amends for what I did and earning my brothers' forgiveness. I can't bring back Ingrid or my father or Gilla, but I can help to get justice for them.'

'What about the assassin you said you killed in Strathclyde? Wasn't that making amends?'

'Not enough. Sandulf found him, I only finished him off. That's why I need to find out the truth behind those pendants. Until I do that, I can't think of myself or of mating. I'm trapped in that day and I can't move on.' He hung his head. 'I don't know how else to explain it.'

'You don't have to. I told you, I know how it feels to lose those you care about.'

'So you did.' He reached a hand out before he could stop himself, grasping her chin between his thumb and forefinger. How could he ever have thought her features were expressionless and impassive? At that moment, her eyes were brimming with emotions—pain, sorrow, sympathy, understanding. Their swirling depths seemed to draw him in…

'Tomorrow,' she murmured, her skin flushing beneath his fingertips before she pulled away finally. 'Tomorrow, if the rain clears, I'll show you.'

Chapter Thirteen

Amazingly, he hadn't asked where they were going. Even more amazingly, he'd barely spoken at all since she'd roused him at dawn with a shake of his good arm and a bowl of porridge, before handing over a pack of supplies and leading the way east. At this time of year they needed to start early if they were going to reach their destination and return again in daylight.

The previous night's storm had cleared the air, leaving blue sky and a smattering of wispy clouds in its wake for their journey through the forest and up into the hills. They made good time, stopping after a couple of hours to eat some of the dried meat the villagers had given her. Danr nodded his thanks though he still didn't speak. It was unnerving. A few days ago, she would have been glad of his silence, but now it felt wrong—*too* unlike him. Was it because of what had happened between them? She'd been trying and failing all morning not to remember the hard feel of his body—such a contrast to the soft touch of his hands—

hoping they could just put it behind them and pretend
that nothing had happened, but to her dismay there was
a new atmosphere of tension between them, one which
made silence even worse. She missed her old talkative
companion—and when had she started to think of him
as a companion?

'We need to go along that ridge and then down the
mountainside,' she announced finally, pointing towards
a jagged stretch of rock between two towering peaks
looming above them. 'It would be quicker to go through
the valley, but we're more likely to bump into Gaels
there. They're used to seeing me, but they're still suspicious of Norsemen.'

'The ridge it is, then.'

She nodded and looked quickly away. On a bright
day like this, his eyes seemed to match the blue sky
behind him. It was strange, but they looked different now—brighter, in some way, than when she'd first
found him. Which made sense since he'd been bleeding
to death at the time, but they seemed deeper somehow,
too. More soulful and intelligent than she'd first given
them, or him, credit for.

'Here.' She passed him a skin filled with water. 'If
we keep up this pace, we'll reach our destination before noon.'

'Good.'

They carried on, climbing up on to the ridge and
then walking along in single file, high enough up to
see the eastern coast of the island, beyond which lay
the sea and beyond that, the coast of Alba itself. The

terrain underfoot was less stable than she remembered, however, uneven and covered in scree.

'Maybe we should consider the valley after all,' Danr called out after a few minutes, pointing ahead to where the ridge tapered so narrowly that one misstep could lead to a potentially deadly fall. 'I don't like the look of that, especially after so much rain.'

'I've walked this way lots of times. We'll go slowly.'

Although, perhaps he had a point, she thought as several stones slid out from beneath her leather shoes and skittered away down the steep slope of the mountain. The thought of walking in uncomfortable silence for any longer than was necessary made her want to continue, but perhaps the rain *had* made it more dangerous. Even Tove and Halvar seemed reluctant to follow them. And if the ridge was so unstable here, then there could be other places ahead that were even worse. Places where it would be too narrow to turn around and go back...

'You're right. We should go—' She was midway through agreeing when the path started to crumble, sending her toppling sideways. Quickly, she flung her weight in the other direction, but it was too late. Her arms were flailing and the very ground beneath her feet was falling away, knocking her legs out from under her and sending her plummeting down the mountainside.

A hand shot out and grabbed her wrist—and not just any hand, she noticed, but a right hand, specifically the one attached to Danr's injured arm. His grasp was firm and unyielding, though it must have been excruciating to hold so much weight. Still, he was doing it, refusing to let go as her body swayed out at a precarious angle above the sheer drop below... Her gaze locked on to his, holding on to that for dear life, too.

'Don't let go,' he muttered between gritted teeth, somewhat unnecessarily, since she had no intention of doing so. At that moment, he was the only thing standing between her and at least a dozen broken bones, if not worse.

'I'm going to lift you back up.' He braced his feet and stretched his other arm out, steadily and cautiously, to grasp her waist. 'Don't move your feet yet, just lean against me.'

She did as he told her, holding her breath as he levered her gently into his arms.

'Now your feet. Slowly.'

'I'm almost there...' She exhaled with relief as she found solid ground again.

'I've got you...' He moved his hands to both sides of her waist as they wobbled. 'But we're still facing the wrong way. I'll need to walk backwards. Can you follow me?'

'Yes.'

'Good.' Despite the circumstances, he gave a reassuring wink. 'Ready?'

She nodded and moved with him, shuffling forward as he took several careful steps back. It wasn't easy, but before long they were back on the wider section of the ridge, almost safe... She was just starting to relax when another section of ground gave way. Thankfully it wasn't much this time, though still enough to send

Danr tumbling on to his back and her flat on to his chest.

'Oomph!' He gave a loud grunt as her forehead smacked against his chin.

'Ow!' She echoed the sentiment, starting to wriggle upwards as she realised she was sprawled on top of him.

'Sissa...' He sucked in a breath.

'What is it?' She froze. 'Are you hurt?'

'No, but...your knee.'

'My... Oh!' She glanced downwards and hurriedly pulled her leg out of his groin, shifting to straddle his thighs instead. 'Sorry.'

'It could have been worse.' His smile was still somewhat pained. 'I hate to say I told you so.'

'You might as well.' She gave a ragged laugh. 'It might be the only time I let you. You just saved my life, Danr.'

'All right, I told you so. That was too close.'

He tightened his arms around her, pulling her back down on to his chest. There was no need for him still to be holding her, a small part of her brain argued, but she didn't resist, lowering her head until she was nestled against him.

'Don't ever scare me like that again,' he murmured, pressing his lips into her hair.

'I'll try not to.' She listened to the wild thump of his heartbeat beneath her ear. It was strangely comforting, a reminder that they were both still alive. No doubt her own heart was racing that fast, too.

'We need to get off this ridge.' He spoke again

after a few moments, though his grip didn't slacken.
'I don't know where our wolf friends have gone, but
they seemed to think this was a bad idea, too.'

'Yes.' She started up, then stopped as he winced
with pain. 'What is it? Your arm?'

'It's all right.'

'No, it's not. Let me take a look.'

'Gladly.' He sat up after her. 'Only let's get off this
ridge first. I was never a great lover of heights.'

'You once told me you used to jump off cliffs into
the sea.'

'I did, but that was just showing off. I never said I
liked it.' He stood and took hold of one of her hands,
clasping it tight as if he were afraid she might fall again
if he didn't hold on. 'Now, let's go.'

That, Danr thought with a shudder, had been altogether too close. For one terrible, heart-stopping moment Sissa had been slipping away from him, falling
beyond his reach down the mountainside. He'd reached
for her wrist without stopping to consider the risk to
himself, though on reflection, it probably hadn't been
the wisest course of action. With the ground crumbling
beneath them, he might easily have fallen with her, but
at the time all he'd known was that there was no way
he was letting her go. Faced with the same choice, he
would do exactly the same thing again. And again. As
many times as she needed for him to save her, even if
he tore his wound open and wrenched his entire arm
off to do it.

Which was exactly what it had felt like.

Stars! He muttered an oath under his breath. His heart was still pounding with fear, not to mention a powerful desire to crush her in his arms and kiss her senseless. His thoughts had been preoccupied all morning with what had happened—*almost* happened—between them during the night, mainly by the fact that he'd desired her so much that he'd been severely tempted to break his vow. But her almost-accident had stirred up feelings in some deeper, more profound part of him. It wasn't *just* desire he felt for her, he realised now. It was…something else. Something he'd never felt before, something truer and more tender, and he had the sudden, alarming conviction that whatever it was, there was no turning back.

And he was *still* holding on to her hand, he realised. Not just that, but his fingers had somehow become entwined with hers, joining their bodies together as if they were one and not two.

'Danr?' She spoke when they reached the base of the valley again. 'Your hand. It's too tight.'

'Too…? Oh.' He frowned and immediately loosened his hold. 'Forgive me.'

'There's nothing to forgive, but you should let me take a look at your arm.'

'It feels better now.'

'I'll be the judge of that. Stop.' She dug her heels in and tugged back against him with surprising force. 'Unfasten your tunic.'

'Later.'

'Now!'

'You can see there's no blood.'

'That's not the point.' She pulled her hand away from his so she could place both of hers on her hips. 'Remember our agreement? You said you'd do whatever I asked. Now, unfasten your tunic or I'll do it myself.'

'Fine.' He heard the catch in his voice as he undid the fastenings at his neck, loosening his mail and tunic and drawing them both down over his injured arm. 'There. Happy now?'

'Not yet. I need to look properly.' She caught his eye for a brief moment, the pupils of her own swelling slightly before she bent her head to examine the wound.

'What do you think?' His voice was a bare rasp of sound, his mind filled with memories from the night before—the feel of her body in his arms, the silken touch of her hair and skin, the scent of herbs and woodsmoke, the sound of moaning as his lips moved over her...

'The wound hasn't opened again,' she murmured, 'though it must have hurt a great deal.'

'I didn't notice.'

'Liar.'

His lips quirked. 'Maybe a little, but I had other things to worry about. I wasn't going to lose you.'

'You might have fallen, too.'

'Then we would have fallen together.'

'Together...' If he wasn't mistaken, her breathing hitched before she cleared her throat. 'We should get on.'

'Why?' He covered her hand with his own as she

drew his tunic back over his shoulder. 'Where are we going? If the journey's so dangerous, why don't you just tell me what happened to you?'

'Because I don't know if I can.' Her face clouded. 'I've never told anyone. I need to show you.'

'All right, but no more pretending to be mountain goats. We stay in the valleys, Gaels or no Gaels.'

'It's a longer route. We'll have to camp overnight.'

'Then we camp overnight.'

'Very well.' She pursed her lips. 'But in that case you have to talk.'

'Are you saying you *want* me to talk?'

'Yes. The quiet was unnerving before, especially after...' Her voice trailed away as a swathe of red crept over her cheeks.

'Ah.' He nodded with comprehension. 'Then I'll talk—*we'll* talk—but I'm leading the way from now on.'

'You don't know where we're going.'

'Good point.' He made a face. 'Then we go side by side. *Together.*'

He readjusted his clothes and they set off again, more slowly and carefully this time, without crossing any more precipices. Tove and Halvar rejoined them after a little while and they remained undisturbed by the Gaels, though he had a suspicion there were eyes watching them on several occasions. Sissa was right; it was a much longer route, but it was far easier to admire the rugged beauty of their surroundings from below. The black peaks looked forbidding and magnificent at the same time, starkly striking as if the earth had been stripped back to its bare essentials, leaving an impression of raw power.

It was halfway through the afternoon when he noticed that Sissa's footsteps were slowing and he guessed they were almost at their destination. There was a faint tang of salt in the air, too, as if they were approaching the other side of the island and the sea again. At last she stopped altogether, pointing towards a rocky overhang in a sheer cliff face.

'That was where Coblaith found me five summers ago.' Her voice sounded tight. 'I was curled up in a ball, sheltering from the cold and rain, shivering so hard I remember my teeth ached from chattering. I doubt I would have survived the night if she hadn't come along when she had. I wasn't even sure I wanted to survive, but I suppose I must have, mustn't I, to have taken shelter in the first place?'

He nodded, walking towards the overhang and placing one hand against the rock. It felt cold and abrasive beneath his fingertips. He had a feeling that saying the wrong thing now might change her mind about showing him more, but the curiosity was almost overwhelming. Perhaps if he asked indirectly?

'What was Coblaith like?'

'She was hard to describe. She never showed a great deal of emotion, but she was kind to me. I think she must have been very beautiful once. She was still striking as an old woman and she never stooped, though her black hair was streaked with white. The first time I saw her I thought she must be a witch. She must have come to see what was happening, what all the noise had been about…' She walked over and put her hand next to his on the rock. 'I should have been afraid of her since I'd been taught never to go near Gaels on my own, but I was beyond fear. She was my only hope.'

'So she saved you?' He moved his hand sideways, touching the tips of his fingers against hers. Somehow just that touch made the rock seem warmer.

'Yes.'

'From what?'

Chapter Fourteen

'From this.' Sissa set down her pack on the hillside, pointing to the half-collapsed, half-burnt remains of her old village below. She hadn't answered Danr's last question, merely leading him to this spot, looking down on to the plateau and beach. He'd told her his story the day before and now she wanted to show him hers—her home, the place where she'd been born and had lived for thirteen years, before she'd fled in horror.

'This was a village.' Danr looked at the scene and then back at her.

'Yes. *My* village. That was our house over there.' She gestured towards a dilapidated timber construction as she made her way down among the ruins. She hadn't visited since the previous spring and, as usual, nature had reclaimed even more of the site in the intervening months. The few remaining buildings were empty shells, held up and almost completely strangled with plants. 'There used to be a dozen or so families living here. Farmers mostly and a few old warriors, though not enough to fight off the raiders.'

'Raiders?' His voice was leaden.

'Yes.' She strove to sound matter of fact about it. 'A group of outlaws by the look of them, though I never knew who they were or where they came from. They just arrived one morning, landing their ships on the beach as if they knew there wasn't much we could do to stop them. Which was true. There wasn't. Our menfolk tried to defend us, but it was no use...' She clamped her lips together for a moment, getting her emotions back under control before continuing. 'They took the little coin we had and all our food supplies for the winter. We might have given it to them if they'd only threatened us, but they were already mad with drink when they arrived. It was as though they were determined on bloodshed.'

'Bastards.' Danr reached down and picked up a small metal object. It looked like the tip of an arrow, the shaft long since rotted away. 'Did they take any prisoners?'

'No.' She had to make a conscious effort to unclench her jaw. 'Everyone was slain. I only escaped because I was coming back with my mother from the river at the time. We saw what was happening from a distance. Then Tove started barking and a warrior noticed and started to run towards us with his sword raised, like this.' She swung her arm above her head, the memory of a battle-crazed warrior flashing through her mind with horrifying clarity.

'What happened?'

She sank her teeth into her bottom lip, lowering her arm again slowly. 'My mother picked up Tove and pushed her into my arms. Then she hugged me and told me to run away and hide.'

'She didn't go with you?'

'No. She picked up some rocks and started to hurl them at the warrior to give me time to get away. It worked. I did what she said and fled up the mountainside. When I looked back, she was already lying on the ground.' She paused for a moment and swallowed. 'I watched the rest from the trees. The outlaws stayed for two days, getting more and more drunk on our ale before loading their ships, burning most of the houses and leaving.'

'Leaving you all alone.' He clenched his jaw. 'It must have been terrible, Sissa. To lose your whole family like that...'

'My parents, yes, but I was their only child, born long after they'd given up hope of having any. I suppose that's a good thing, that I had no brothers or sisters to mourn, but the whole village had been like a family to me. I mourned everyone.'

'I'm sorry.'

'So am I.' She took a deep breath. 'I'm sorry for what happened to your family, too. I didn't express it well yesterday. I couldn't. It all sounded too familiar.'

'At least I still have my brothers. I can't imagine what it must have been like to be all alone. How long was it until Coblaith found you?'

'A few days. At first Tove looked after me.' She

threw an affectionate glance towards the wolf. 'She kept the other animals at bay and brought me food.'

'Your mother was wise.'

'Yes. She wanted me to survive so I did. That's *why* I did, for her, not for me.' She shuddered. 'After the raiders left all I wanted was to lie down in the dirt at my mother's side and never get up. Instead, I laid stones over her body and cried. It was all I could do.'

She turned and looked out across the sea to the hills of the mainland beyond. 'You asked me once if I was lonely. I was *then*. Coblaith was company of a sort, but we couldn't talk and then she left, too. There were times when I thought I might go mad. Then the new Norsemen came and built the village where your enemy lives now. I watched them do it and thought about going there. One day I went closer for a look, but the people thought I was a ghost and ran away.' She gave a tight laugh. 'Maybe I should have brushed my hair first.'

He didn't laugh back. 'Why didn't you tell them who you were?'

'I couldn't.'

'Couldn't?'

'I couldn't speak. I tried, but it was as though my voice had become trapped inside me. I couldn't say a word.' She smiled sadly. 'I don't know whether it was because I'd become so used to *not* speaking or because I had doubts about being there, but that's when I knew it was too late for me to go back. I knew I could never live among people again. I could never be a part of their world. Then I realised that it was useful for them to be afraid of me. I knew that their fear and the forest would keep me safe.'

'And you've been keeping yourself safe ever since?'

'Yes.' She nodded. 'My voice came back after a while, but I didn't use it very often, only with Tove occasionally. Now nobody comes near me except when they're sick or injured, then they always hurry away.' She paused. 'Everyone except you. You're the only one who wouldn't go away, the only person I've spoken to properly in five years.'

'Then I'm honoured...' he inclined his head slightly '...and sorry. For forcing you to speak that day.'

'You made me so angry, I couldn't help shouting at you.'

'I'm good at provoking people.' He looked regretful. 'But if I'd known what you'd been through, I would never have done it.'

'Part of me is glad that you did. It feels good to talk again, just for a while.'

'But there's still one thing I don't understand. How did you end up helping the villagers if they're so scared of you?'

'One day about two years ago I came across a man who'd been gored by a stag. The people around him were mending the wound badly so I did it for them. I think they didn't dare stop me. Then a few days later, someone came to the edge of the forest and hung a necklace from one of the trees. Ever since then, people have been coming to me for help and giving me food and clothing in return. That's why I go to the edge of the forest every so often.'

'But maybe you could speak to them now?' He caught her hand, holding it between his. 'You could explain all this to them the way you have to me. You don't need to worry about the same thing happening again. There are more people here now, more warriors to defend the village. You could be safe there.'

'Nowhere is safe, not really—besides, why should I trust *them*? I've seen what people are capable of. Warriors...' She looked down at their joined hands, feeling a chill despite the warmth of his skin. 'The forest is my home. I know how to survive here.'

'But you can do more than survive. There should be more to life than survival, Sissa. You could go—'

'*No!*' she interrupted him, squeezing his hand until he fell silent. 'This is who I am and where I belong. If there had been a way for me to find out who those raiders were and get justice for my family, I would have taken it, but there wasn't. But if there is for you, then I want to help.'

'What?' His shoulders stiffened visibly. 'What do you mean?'

'I mean that *you* might not be able to go to the village and confront your stepmother, but I can. *I* can show her those pendants and find out the truth.'

Danr held himself very still, shocked into silence by her words, by their surroundings, by *all* of it. He'd suspected that something terrible had happened in her past, yet the idea of another massacre had never occurred to him. It was so similar to his own story and yet somehow even worse. At least he'd been a grown man in Maerr, but she'd been little more than a child, watching the slaughter of everyone she knew in the world before being left to survive almost completely alone in the wild for five years... And now she was offering to help him—*him* of all people! As if he were worthy of her help. As if he were the one who'd suffered the most! He wanted to wrap her tight in his arms and then track down every last member of that raiding party and get justice for her, too.

'No.' He shook his head. 'It's too dangerous.'

'Only for you.' She thrust her jaw out. 'You said that you didn't show your stepmother the pendants when you first confronted her, didn't you?'

'No. I mentioned them, but I never showed her.'

'Then let me do it. Maybe I'll be able to tell something from her reaction.'

'She knows I'm on the island somewhere. She'll assume I gave them to you.'

'*Or* she'll think I found them on your body and simply took them. It doesn't matter. She'll be frightened enough that I know they're hers. She'll think I have some power to see the truth.' She shrugged. 'She can ask me whatever she wants; I won't answer.'

'She might hold you prisoner until you *do* tell her.'

'The people in the village won't let her. They value my help and they're frightened of me, remember? They'll be afraid I might summon a storm in revenge.'

'There's still Joarr. He didn't look very frightened of you yesterday.'

'No...' Her face clouded slightly. 'But he won't be

able to go against the wishes of his kinsman, no matter what he wants to do with me. Trust me, Danr.'

'It's not a matter of trust. It's about your safety. I don't want you going anywhere near either of them.'

She wrenched her hand away. 'Why not?'

'Because this is my task, not yours.'

'I'm offering to help you.'

'I don't want help.'

'But you *need* it.'

'Sissa…' He took another step towards her. 'I'm grateful for the offer, but I don't want you taking any risks, especially for me.'

'I won't—'

'No!' He spoke in a tone of command. 'I won't change my mind about this. You just said that you're safe in the forest because people leave you alone. Well, if you get tangled up in my mess then they might *not* leave you alone any more. I won't ruin your life. You've already done enough for me. I don't deserve any more.'

'You deserve justice, if you can get it.' She folded her arms, her expression stubborn. 'And you need a better plan than holding a sword to your stepmother's throat and hoping she confesses.'

'I know.'

'And you haven't thought of one…'

'Not yet.'

'So you have to admit that my plan is a good one…'

'That's not the point. I'll think of something else.'

'All right.' She let out an exasperated-sounding sigh. 'I won't go.'

Danr watched as she turned and walked away. She

was right, it *was* a good plan, only there was no way in hell he was going to let her go through with it. He didn't want any more lives on his conscience, especially not hers. His chest constricted with a painful tightness just at the thought. If *anything* were to happen to her, he didn't know what he'd do...

He took a deep breath, trying to control the feeling. A few shafts of evening sunlight had broken through the clouds, bathing the scene in an orange-gold glow. Sissa was just ahead of him, looking so slender and vulnerable, walking amidst the ruins of her former home, yet she'd proven herself stronger and tougher than most warriors he'd known. He doubted many of them could have survived in the wild on their own for so long. Or had the strength of mind to bear it either. He didn't think *he* would have been able to. Whereas she... He felt a rush of tenderness. *She* was independent, indomitable and invincible, with a spine made of finely tempered steel and a pair of grey eyes that seemed to penetrate through to his very core. Looking at her now, she struck him as the most beautiful, desirable woman he'd ever laid eyes on. How could he *not* have seen that at the start? He desired her in a way he'd never desired anyone before and not just because it had been so long since he'd lain with a woman, but because his heart wanted her, too. Unworthy as he was, he wanted to be *with* her as much as he wanted to bed her. Because he loved her. He'd never expected to feel the emotion, had always distrusted it, but now that he did, it made him feel clean inside somehow, exhilarated even, as if he *could* be worthy of her some day. He was in love with her.

And he'd sworn an oath that meant he had to leave as soon as he was able...

He clenched his jaw and shifted his attention to their surroundings. The outline of the half-destroyed village was mostly hidden by brambles and nettles, but the positions of the old houses were still clear if you knew how to look.

'It's a good site for a village.' He came to stand beside Sissa. She was on the edge of the shore, looking out at the waves. The sea and sky were almost the same colour now, a darkening slate-blue. If it hadn't been for the hills of the mainland in the distance they might both have merged into one.

'It is...' she twisted to look at him '...but people are afraid to come here. Even the Gaels think it's haunted.'

He nodded with understanding. He couldn't blame anyone for that. He'd never felt the same about Maerr after the massacre. 'Don't you?'

'No, but if it were then I don't believe the ghosts of my family would ever hurt me.' She heaved a sigh. 'But I wouldn't want anyone to build here either.'

'Over there, then.' He pointed further along the shore to where the land rose up to a plateau. 'That would be a good site.'

'Are *you* looking for a new home, Norseman?'

He blinked as she turned to look fully at him, her golden hair blowing around her shoulders and glowing copper-red in the fading sunlight. He'd often thought of it as a cloak and now it looked more like one than ever... He held his breath, trying to fix the image in his mind. At that moment he could almost believe that the rest of the world didn't exist, that there was only the two of them, that Hilda and Joarr held no importance for him, that he had no oath to fulfil, that he was a free man...

Was he looking for a home? The question seemed to echo around his head. He was a man who'd spent most of his life living for the moment, never considering the future, never looking for anything resembling commitment. Then after the massacre he'd never allowed himself to think beyond fulfilling his oath, but what *would* he do if and when he finally redeemed himself in his brothers' eyes? Where would he go? To Rurik in Glannoventa? Alarr in Eireann? Sandulf in Strathclyde? None of those ideas sounded very appealing any more. Not compared to a rain-soaked, mist-covered island and the wild-haired woman who lived there.

But she wanted to be on her own, away from people, away from warriors especially. Unless he could persuade her otherwise...and then prove himself worthy.

'Not yet.' He felt a new sense of determination. 'Just a place to camp. It'll be dark soon.'

Chapter Fifteen

'What are you doing?' Sissa sat down beside the fire, looking quizzically at the knife and block of wood in Danr's hands.

'Carving *tafl* pieces.' He leaned back against his pack with a grin. 'I thought I could make us a set so we could play. The board isn't a problem, but these are tricky. Rurik was always better at carving things. He has more patience than me, but I'm going to try.'

'They look good to me.' She started to smile back and then froze, struck by a strange tingling sensation, like fingers stroking the back of her neck. They'd set up camp in a cove adjacent to her old village, him building a fire, her catching some fish, then him cooking them while she'd sat with her arm around Tove, watching. She'd just been to collect some fresh water and now she was almost ready for bed. Despite the turmoil and tumult of the day it all felt so…comfortable. *Too* comfortable. Not only was he spoiling her for anyone else's cooking, including her own, but she was start-

ing to grow accustomed to companionship again, as if
he were truly her mate. It was disorientating. Coming
back to the site of her old village had been painful in
one way, reminding her of how it felt to lose the people
she loved, but it had been bittersweet in another, calling up memories of how it felt to love and be loved.
It made her wonder what it would be like to open her
heart again. Was it even possible after so long? Did
she want it to be?

Her body went rigid at the thought. Danr *wasn't* her
mate and he never could be. She'd let him further into
her life than she'd ever intended, but she couldn't—
wouldn't—let herself fall in love with him. She lived
on her own. That was the way her life was and the
way it had to be. And even if she *could* let herself fall
in love with him, he was only staying with her for a
short while, until his arm recovered, no longer. After
that, he had to do what he'd come to Skíð to do: confront his stepmother and possibly get himself killed
in the attempt. Even if he survived, he'd still be leaving. She had to keep on telling herself that, no matter
how much she enjoyed his company and he seemed
to like hers, *or* how curious he made her, *or* that he'd
saved her life that day, *or* that she trusted him enough
to show him her village…

No, there was no future for them, she told herself
as she reached into her pack and drew out a comb. She
wouldn't let herself be tempted.

'Here. Let me do that.'

Before she knew what happening, Danr had put
down his knife and was crouching beside her, taking

the comb from her hand and pulling it gently through her hair.

'Wh-what are you doing?' She twisted around, startled.

'Combing your hair.' He put his other hand on the top of her head, turning her to face the front again. 'Trust me, I'm good at it.'

'But…' She started to protest, then closed her eyes as his hand followed the comb downwards, stroking her head the same way he stroked Halvar. It felt surprisingly—wonderfully—soothing. Blissful, in fact, making her feel relaxed all over.

'That's not so bad, is it?' There was a smile in his voice.

'No.' She gave a contented sigh. 'What about your carving?'

'I've another twenty-three pieces to go anyway.'

'Oh.' She fought to repress a smile. 'You know, I'm not sure I remember the rules of *tafl*.'

'I'll remind you.' The comb caught on a knot, but he untangled it deftly.

'You still might not have time to carve all the pieces. You'll be able to wield a sword soon enough, then you'll get the answers you want and leave. You don't want to be stuck on Skíð over the winter.'

'Don't I? It's not so bad here.'

'You won't think so when the snows come.'

'*You* manage.'

'I'm used to it, but you'll still need to leave before then. You said your brothers were expecting you in Eireann.'

'Ye-es, but the truth is, I like it here. I still have an oath to fulfil, but after I've done that, perhaps I could come back?'

'Come back?' Her voice sounded alarmingly high-pitched. The idea made her feel tempted and panic-stricken at the same time. 'Won't that depend on how things go with your stepmother? She might not want you here.'

'No, but I don't suppose she wanders around the forest very often. I could come back and build myself a tree house.'

'That sounds cold. Where would you put the hearth?'

'Good point. That would be just for the summer then. In the winter, I'd build another roundhouse.'

'You want to live in the forest? I thought warriors all wanted their own halls?'

'I've spent enough of my life in great halls and I never particularly wanted to be a warrior. I just want a home...' The comb stilled briefly. 'I suppose I always thought I'd end up wherever Rurik was, but now I'm not so sure any more. I feel peaceful here. I feel peaceful with you. I know you don't want to be around people, but would one person really be so bad? What do you think, Sissa? Would you object if I came back after I've fulfilled my oath?'

She sucked in a breath at the question. *Would* she object if he came back? He made it sound as if he wanted to come back to *her*. She didn't know how to answer, especially when her heart and head were giving such conflicting opinions.

'That still sounds strange.' She changed the subject instead.

'What? Your name?'

'Yes. I thought I didn't ever want to hear it again, that it would remind me too much of my parents, but I like it.'

'Then I'll keep saying it, Sissa. Would you pass me that chunk of bread please, Sissa? I'd be very grateful, Sissa.'

She rolled her eyes and reached for the bread. 'I'm going to run out of supplies *before* winter at this rate. You eat like an ox.'

'And you don't eat enough. That's why this is for you. Here.' He tore off a chunk and placed it back in her hands. 'Food isn't just about survival, it's about pleasure.'

'What does pleasure have to do with it?'

He sighed. 'You know, somewhere between the two of us is probably the right balance. My life has been too much about pleasure and yours has been too little.'

She made a harrumphing sound, accepting the bread and taking a bite.

'It applies to other things, too,' he carried on, still combing. '*You've* been too independent while I've relied on people too much.'

'*You* talk all the time…'

'…and *you* haven't spoken enough. We're two extremes. We should either hate each other or—' He stopped before he could finish the sentence. 'Well, we can be friends anyway.'

'Yes.' Her throat seemed very dry all of a sudden.

The way his hand was caressing her hair felt more than *friendly*...

'Could you tell me another story?' she asked, stalling for time again.

'So you *do* like my stories.' He sounded pleased by the request. 'In that case, do you know the one about Kjarten, the warrior prince who defeated Uradech, the great troll of Alba, using just one finger?'

'No.'

'Neither do I. Shame.'

'Very funny.' She reached an arm behind her back to swat at him. 'A *real* story.'

'All right. This one is about Fell, the blacksmith who forged golden rings so beautiful that all the princesses in all the lands wanted to marry him.'

'Just so they could have beautiful rings?'

'I expect he made other things, too. Bracelets and necklaces probably. Some women value such things.' He chuckled. 'Of course he was tempted. Who wouldn't be? But his heart yearned for another, a thrall named Astrid who cared naught for gold or jewellery.'

'I like the sound of her. Did she care for him?'

'Oh, yes. Conveniently, he was a very handsome blacksmith.'

'Then why didn't he just buy her with one of his rings?'

'Well, now you've spoiled the ending.'

'What? Ow!' She twisted her head sharply, causing the comb to snag on another tangle. 'If that was the whole story, it wasn't a very good one.'

'Alas, the life of a skald... Everyone has an opinion.'

'Tell me a proper story this time or...' She pursed her lips, trying to think of a punishment. 'Or I won't let you comb my hair any more.'

'Ah, well, in that case...' He was quiet for a few moments, thinking while the comb continued to skim through her hair, the strokes becoming longer and surer as the tangles unravelled.

'All right, I have one. There was once a woman who lived on her own in the forest. People were afraid of her because they didn't know who she was or where she'd come from. Some of them thought she was a ghost. Her heart had been broken once, but it was still a good heart, a caring one. She helped people when they were hurt and healed them when they were sick, though she never breathed as much as a word. Then one day a warrior came. His heart was broken, too, but it wasn't such a good heart. He'd done bad things in his past, but she healed him anyway. She made him feel hopeful again.' She felt him lean closer, whispering the final words in her ear. 'For which he was very grateful, even if he didn't deserve it.'

She swallowed, the skin on her neck tingling as his breath warmed it. 'Everyone deserves a second chance.'

'What about a third or fourth one?' He put the comb aside and moved around in front of her, crouching down so their eyes were level. 'Maybe some of us have used up all our chances. Maybe I used mine up even before the massacre. Maybe I've done too much to be forgiven. Some days it feels like too much. Sometimes I actually wish I was still the shallow man I used to be. Then maybe I could forget, but I can't. That's why I need to fulfil my oath. Until I do that, I'm trapped by the consequences of who I was.'

'You mean because of all your women?' she couldn't stop herself from asking. 'Did you really behave so badly?'

'Worse than that.'

'Just to entertain your father? To get his attention?'

'Not *just*, no. As much as I'd like to blame him entirely, I enjoyed being the irresponsible joker of the family. It made me stand out. I enjoyed being the Jarl's son, too. It had advantages.'

'You didn't love any of your women, then?'

He shook his head. 'I thought love was for fools. I saw what it did to my mother. I was always determined not to end up the same way.'

'But weren't you angry about that? Weren't you furious at your father for the way he treated her?'

His jaw tightened. 'It's complicated. When I was younger I didn't really understand what had happened between them, but as I grew up...yes, I was angry at him. I still am.'

'Did you ever tell him?'

'No. He wasn't the kind of man you could tell things to. Or maybe I was afraid he would banish me if I dared to criticise him. I already felt as if Rurik and I didn't belong. I didn't want us to lose what position we had. Maybe I was afraid of being cast out and left all alone. Or maybe I was just a shallow good-for-nothing and I chose not to think about it. Either way, what kind of man does that make me? To crave attention from the man who ruined my mother's life?'

'A young and foolish one, perhaps? You were only a boy when your mother died and he was still your father. Maybe you just wanted a place to belong and be loved. All children want that, don't they?'

'Adults, too.'

Her gaze flickered. 'You just said you thought love was for fools.'

'I also said I was a shallow good-for-nothing back then. I've learned a few things over the past three years. I can't make excuses for my behaviour, but I know I'm not that man any more. A place to belong and be loved is all I want now. Maybe it was all I ever wanted, deep down.'

She hesitated, gazing into his eyes for the space of half a dozen heartbeats. 'It sounds like all we might want, but adults know life isn't so simple. You know my parents used to sit outside our house on evenings like this. They wouldn't talk. They would just sit and look at the view, resting after the day's work. I used to sit with them, at their feet. Those were perfect moments. Moments of love and peace and beauty. I remember being happy. But it was all an illusion. It was all taken away in a few minutes.'

'It doesn't mean that those moments weren't real. Love and peace and beauty all still exist. There are good people in the world as well as bad ones. You can be happy again.'

She bit her lip and looked out towards the sea. 'I'm better off on my own. Safer.'

'Safety isn't happiness.'

'No, but it's important.'

'Sissa…' He dipped his head as if he agreed with her, though when he looked up again, the look in his eyes took her breath away. 'You might be right, but maybe we both deserve a second chance. I might not be worthy of one, but I want to be. I don't know if it will be possible, or how long it will take, but if I survive to fulfil my oath to my brothers then I'd like to come back here, to you, if you'll have me?'

'You mean…as a mate?'

'As whatever you want.'

He leaned forward and pressed his lips against hers. Unlike their previous kisses, it was chaste and light and so brief that it seemed to come and go in a moment, yet somehow felt more powerful than all the others combined. She put her hands on his shoulders, her mind and body in turmoil, trying to unravel the tangle of her thoughts. Could she allow him to come back? Could she risk a second chance at happiness?

'I don't know. I need to think.' Her voice was still strangely high-pitched. 'We should get some rest.'

'Good idea.' There was a waver in his voice, too. 'Your bed awaits.'

She looked towards the pile of ferns he'd gathered earlier. 'That's for me?'

'Of course. Do you think I made it for myself?' He laid his cloak over the top. 'Now come here and let me tuck you in.'

She did as he instructed, sitting down cautiously and then stretching out on top of his cloak. 'It's quite comfortable.'

'Good.' He took the edges of the cloak and wrapped them around her. 'Warm enough?'

'Yes.'

'No twigs in unfortunate places?'

She laughed. 'None, but what about you? You'll get cold without your cloak.'

'I have a blanket in my pack.' He shrugged. 'It's not that cold.'

'As long as you're sure...' She sighed.

'I'm sure. I might not know much about shelters, but beds are my specialty.' He bent down, cupping her cheek in his hand and gazing into her face so intently that for a moment she thought he was going to kiss her again. She held her breath, unsure whether she wanted him to or not, but then his lips brushed her forehead and he turned away. 'Goodnight, Sissa.'

'Goodnight.'

She watched him lie down by the fireside. *Could* she allow him to come back? It felt too risky somehow, yet it wasn't so much of a risk, surely? He wasn't asking her to love him, or saying that he loved her either, and she had no intention of opening her own heart again—not yet anyway. All he was asking for was permission to come back. *Could* she give it to him?

'Good morning, sleepyhead.' Danr buckled his sword belt around his waist, watching appreciatively as Sissa sat up and pushed aside the curtain of tangles over her face. 'How do you make your hair so wild just by sleeping on it? I might have to comb it again. Sleep well?'

'Very well.' She stretched her arms out to the sides. 'Your bed was very comfortable.'

'Good.' He forced himself to look away although he could have spent several minutes just standing, watching her. Last night had been the first time in his life that he'd tucked a woman into bed and simply wished her goodnight. He'd never kissed or been kissed so chastely either, at least not since his mother, yet he'd meant it with every fibre of his being.

'It really is beautiful here.' He put his hands on his hips and looked out at the sea and the isle of Alba beyond. 'It's a shame to leave.'

He meant that, too. All in all, it really did feel like a shame to leave. He felt more refreshed than he had for a long time. Their conversation the previous evening had given him hope for the future. If he wasn't a lost cause then maybe there *was* a future for him, after all...with *her.* He'd never thought of himself as the kind of man who could settle down with one woman, but with Sissa the idea was actually appealing. More than that, it was what he wanted. What would his brothers think if they could see him now? he wondered, grinning like some besotted youth. They wouldn't believe it. *He* almost couldn't believe it. It had all happened so quickly, but he knew his feelings were true. The bright light of day had brought clarity to his thoughts, allowing him to finally see a way forward. He couldn't tell her he loved her yet, not while he still had an oath to fulfil, but he would and soon. He'd finally found the place where he belonged. Once he'd confronted Hilda and earned his brothers' forgiveness, then he could be her mate in truth, if she'd have him.

Would she have him? She hadn't given him permission to come back, but she hadn't refused him either. That gave him hope and if there was one thing he'd always been good at, it was persuading women to do things. He had a feeling that Sissa was going to be a greater challenge than all the rest put together, but he was determined.

He rolled his shoulders, seized with a sense of purpose and resolve. He was going to fulfil his oath, then he was going to come back, tell the woman he loved how he felt and persuade her to let him stay.

'Come on.' He tossed her a flask. 'We can eat on the way.'

She looked up in surprise. 'I thought you just said it was a shame to leave?'

'It is, but we have an island to cross and I have a stepmother to speak to.'

'Now? What about your arm?'

'If I can hold you over the edge of a mountain, then my arm is recovered enough to fight.'

'*Fight*?' Surprise turned to alarm.

'Only if I have to, but hopefully it won't come to that. I've decided to do what you said and take a branch of peace to the village.'

'You said that Joarr would probably kill you anyway. What if he challenges you?'

He made a face. 'Then I'll try my best to dissuade him. I did some thinking last night, about all the things you said about Hilda and how it didn't make sense that she was involved in the massacre. I think perhaps you might be right. That day on the beach when I fought Joarr, she held him back. I didn't understand why at the time, but maybe I *can* talk to her. At the very least, I'm going to try.'

'But so soon?'

'The sooner the better.' He smiled and threw his pack over his shoulder. The sooner he left, the sooner he could come back and seize his second chance at happiness—with her.

Chapter Sixteen

'**C**arving again?'

Danr lifted his head with a smile at the sound of Sissa's voice. They'd arrived back at the roundhouse around twilight, just in time to light a fire before darkness descended completely.

'What do you think? I'm quite pleased with this one. It's supposed to be a king.'

'It's very good.' She sat down on the ground beside him. 'I thought you said you weren't patient enough for carving?'

'I know. I'm surprising myself.'

'Well, here's your reward.' She passed him a bottle. 'You've earned it.'

'What is it?' He pulled open the stopper and sniffed. 'Mead?'

'Yes. Sometimes the villagers give it to me.'

He stared at her, trying to decide whether to be pleased or annoyed. 'You mean you've had mead this whole time and *not* told me?'

'You haven't been here *that* long.'

'It's still a long time without mead!'

She rolled her eyes. 'I prefer fresh water from the mountain.'

'Good.' He lifted the bottle to his lips and took a long draught. 'That means more of this for me.'

'There might be some wine in the cave.'

'*Might* be?' He threw her an exasperated look and took another swig. She was right; he *had* earned it after their second long hike in as many days. More than that, he needed it, if only to dampen any impulse he might feel to visit her roundhouse in the middle of the night again. Exhausted as he was, being back here, so close to the place where they'd lain together during the storm, made his trousers feel uncomfortably tight. He had to keep stopping himself from thinking about the way she'd looked that night, the way she'd felt beneath him, too… He was tempted to ask whether she'd made a decision about him staying yet, but he had a strong suspicion that rushing her wouldn't do any good. Maybe he ought to wait until after he'd confronted Hilda anyway…

She gave a wide yawn and stretched her legs out in front of her, propping herself up on her elbows as she looked up at the sky. 'The *norðrljós* are bright tonight.'

'They are.' He tipped his head back to gaze upwards. The white streaks and swirls were breathtakingly beautiful, stretching and shimmering in ever-changing patterns as if the currents of the sea surrounding the island were being reflected in the sky above their heads.

'There was a streak of blue a few moments ago. We see that often in Maerr.'

'Really?' She sounded wistful. 'I've only seen green lights a handful of times. Once I thought I saw purple, too, but it was gone so quickly I wondered afterwards if I'd imagined it. I love to watch them, though. It looks like the sky is dancing.' She paused and glanced across at him. 'Have you thought any more about my offer of help?'

'No.' His brows snapped together at once. 'And I'm not going to.'

'You should.'

'I told you, I'm taking a branch of peace and going alone. I don't want you in any danger.'

'But you agreed that she might not have been involved in the massacre, and if she wasn't then it's *not* dangerous for me to go.'

'*Might* isn't a very convincing argument. I still don't want you involved. I'm going to the village tomorrow—*alone.*'

She glared at him. 'Why not the day after tomorrow?'

He lifted an eyebrow, pleased by the thought that she didn't want him to leave. 'Trying to keep me here?'

'It's not that.' She tilted her chin up. 'I just have a few more jobs for you to do first. You promised to repay me for all my help, remember?'

'Ah, so I did. All right, one more day. Then I can do a thorough search of that cave. If there's anything else to drink, I'll find it.'

'Fine.' A faintly guilty expression crossed her face for a moment before her jaw dropped. 'Look!'

'What is it?' He twisted around as she pointed behind him.

'Red! Over there!'

'Pink, too. Well, I've never seen that before.'

'Neither have I. It's spectacular.'

He turned to look down at her again. 'How could anyone prefer a hall? What kind of hall could provide all of this? It's perfect.'

'You're not even looking now.'

'I'm looking.' He smiled. 'Trust me, Sissa, I'm looking.'

Sissa rose silently at dawn. Her intention had been to persuade Danr by giving him the mead and letting it befuddle his senses enough that he would agree to her plan, but since that *hadn't* happened, she'd decided it was time to resort to more underhand methods.

Fortunately, the ale had had other useful effects. He was still slumbering peacefully beside the fire, oblivious to the world as she wrapped a fur cloak around her shoulders and crouched down beside him, reaching for the leather pouch he always wore around his neck. Gently, she lifted it up, taking care not to pull as she sliced a knife through the cord and then drew it away.

Stars! She breathed a sigh of relief and peeked inside, making sure the three pendants were still nestled there before setting off, Tove at her heels. She knew the way to the village even in darkness, making her way swiftly through the trees as the sun rose slowly over the sky. She needed to hurry and get there before Danr woke up, guessed where she'd gone and followed her, though with any luck he'd assume that she was bathing and wouldn't notice the loss of the pouch until much later.

She felt a twinge of guilt about taking something so precious to him, not to mention going behind his back, but she had confidence in her plan and his sudden decision to confront Hilda sooner rather than later had decided her. Her plan was the safest option—certainly better than him going to confront Hilda and ending up fighting Joarr if he lost his temper again—and it was her decision if she wanted to go through with it, not his. Admittedly, it was *his* business, but hadn't he foisted himself on to *her* life? She could do the same thing if she wanted. She wasn't sure whether the second chance he spoke about was possible, but she knew with every fibre of her being that she didn't want him to get hurt. Which meant that she had to act before he did.

She stopped on the edge of the wood and put her hand on Tove's head as a signal for her to stay. She'd never been inside the village before, but somehow she doubted the inhabitants would react well to the sight of a wolf. She didn't know how they'd react to her either, but there was only one way to find out… She reached into the leather pouch for the pendants, curled her fingers around them and then walked up to the gates on her own. They were still closed, but, judging by the incredulous expression on the face of the guard on top of the wooden palisade, her arrival had been noticed.

She tapped her foot impatiently as he shouted something over his shoulder and then disappeared for a few seconds. Fortunately, it wasn't long before the large gates creaked open and he reappeared with another guard, both of them clutching spears and wearing part-threatening, part-nervous expressions.

She pursed her lips with grim humour. She supposed she couldn't blame them. Her appearance seemed to alarm the villagers at the best of times, but a dawn arrival at their gates was even eerier than usual. On the other hand, it could be useful. She *wanted* an atmosphere of tension. Now she just had to hope that Hilda was already awake.

She lifted her chin and walked between the middle of the two guards, aware of their spears following behind as she made her way through the village and towards the great longhouse in the centre. This was where Knut, their leader, lived along with his wife, Alva, whose fever after the birth of their last child she'd successfully treated the previous summer. Hopefully Knut would still be grateful to her for that. At least enough not to chase her away, as the guards at her heels—there appeared to be at least half a dozen of them now—seemed to wish to do.

At last she reached the longhouse and stopped. There was already a sound of commotion inside, of raised voices and benches being pushed back, then Knut himself appeared, his red hair unkempt as if he'd just been roused from his bed, along with Alva, Joarr and another woman she'd never seen close up, a woman with dark braided hair and a certain look of hardness around her eyes.

This, Sissa assumed, was Hilda, the stepmother who'd made Danr feel unwelcome for most of his life. She'd thought about asking him for a more detailed physical description the evening before, but then changed her mind in case it aroused his suspicions. The woman in front of her, however, appeared to be around the right age with a few threads of grey streaking her hair and clothes fine enough to suggest that she was, or had once been, a great lady. So far, so good...

'Lady.' Knut took a few steps towards her and bowed his head. 'You're welcome here.'

She made no move to acknowledge him, narrowing her eyes on Hilda instead. By the way Joarr moved to try to block her view, she knew she had the right person. Even better... Slowly, she lifted a hand and pointed towards her.

'What is this?' Joarr took a threatening step forward, but Knut turned his head sharply.

'Keep back!'

'Why is she pointing?' It was Hilda who spoke this time, her voice cracking slightly as Sissa crooked a finger and beckoned for her to come closer. 'What does she want with me?'

'Don't move.' Joarr put a hand on her arm.

'Let her go.' Knut spoke in an undertone. 'Hilda will be safe.'

'No. I don't like it.'

'It's what the healer wants.'

'It's all right, Joarr.' Hilda removed his hand herself and took a few cautious steps forward, her face tight with anxiety.

When she was within reaching distance, Sissa slowly unfurled her fingers, revealing the three arrow pendants in her palm. The other woman let out a horrified gasp and recoiled, her face blanching instantly.

'Where did you get those?'

Sissa didn't respond, keeping her eyes fixed on her face instead. There was shock there, yes, horror even, but guilt? No, if anything she looked more confused than guilty...

'What is it? A threat?' Joarr shoved his way past Knut and strode forward, his nostrils flaring as he looked at the arrows in her hand. 'What do they mean?'

'They're my pendants.' Hilda's eyes were wide. 'The ones Sigurd gave me after our sons were born. I'd know them anywhere, but I don't understand...' She grabbed hold of his sleeve, tugging him closer and murmuring so softly that Sissa could barely make out the words.

'Tell us how you came by these.' Joarr looked up again, his expression like granite. 'Did you steal them?'

'Joarr.' Knut's voice was heavy with warning. 'You will not accuse her, not here in my village.'

'I want some answers.'

'Maybe so, but she's our healer and she's valuable to us. She cures our people when they're sick. She cured my wife. You will not offend her.'

There were a few seconds of tense silence while Joarr continued to glare, before he grasped Hilda's arm and pulled her back towards the hall. 'As you wish.'

'Lady.' Knut gave her a strained-looking smile. 'Forgive my kinsman. He meant no insult, but we don't understand. If you could explain somehow…or show us more…?'

She didn't answer, levelling one last look at Hilda before turning on her heel and walking back towards the gates. *There*, it was done. She'd achieved what she'd come for. She had the answer Danr wanted and more besides…but she could feel Joarr's gaze burning a hole in her back the whole way.

Chapter Seventeen

'What do you want?' Danr pushed Halvar's muzzle out of his face as the wolf nudged and then licked him awake. 'Is it time for *dagmal* already? You know we have to bathe first. It's the rule.'

He gave a wide yawn and folded his good arm behind his head, resisting the urge to scratch the other one where his scar was itching. The sky above his head was greyer than yesterday and, if he wasn't mistaken, there was a hint of moisture in the air, doubtless a prelude to heavier rain, but the sun was already higher than he'd expected. He must have slept longer because of the mead…

'We'll wait for our womenfolk to come back, shall we?' He smiled at the thought of Sissa and Tove. 'What tasks do you think she'll have for me today? Catching a stag with my bare hands? Wrestling a wild boar? Or maybe…'

He stopped, struck with the sudden, sharp impression that something wasn't right. It wasn't anything about his surroundings either. The world around him looked the same as it had the previous night. No, it was something closer, something about *him*, something that felt different… He lifted a hand to his chest, though it still took him a few more seconds to locate the source, or rather the absence of a source.

What? He fumbled around his neck as if he might be imagining things, but the leather pouch was definitely gone. Not just that, but the cord it hung from, too.

'Sissa!' He roared her name, already knowing it wouldn't do any good. She was the only one who could have taken it and he knew exactly the reason why!

He was on his feet in a second, strapping on his sword belt and sprinting out of the clearing. He could feel his heart pounding in his ears as well as his chest, like a hammer against an anvil as he leapt over rocks and fallen branches, hurtling through the forest like a madman, Halvar at his side. If he'd had any doubts about his feelings for Sissa before, he knew what they were now. If she'd put herself in danger, then he'd fight until the last breath left his body to save her. He'd take on every man in the village and more; he'd fight Joarr one-handed; he'd tear the whole place apart… Thoughts of violence coursed through his head, none of them quite able to distract from the fear gripping his chest.

He was running so fast he almost charged headlong into her. She was looking over her shoulder, unaware of him at first either, so that he had to dodge quickly to one side, skidding to a halt just before he barrelled into a ditch.

'Sissa,' he gasped her name, relief flooding through him as he braced his hands on his knees in an attempt to get his breath back. 'You…where…what were you…?'

'I've been to the village.' She glanced back in the direction she'd come from. 'But we need to get away from here. Hurry.'

'Why?' He jerked upright again, gripping his sword hilt and drawing the blade halfway from its scabbard. 'Is someone following you?'

'I'm not sure. I don't think so.' Her brows lowered. 'It's just a feeling. Your old friend Joarr doesn't trust me.'

'Did he say so? Did he threaten you?'

'No, but I don't trust him either.' She touched his arm as if they were just out for a morning stroll. 'Come on. We'll cross the river and then climb part of the way up the mountain in case he tries to track us.'

'I should stay and fight him.' Danr glowered through the trees. 'I'm ready.'

'What would be the point?' She put her hands on her hips with an exasperated look. 'I went there to *stop* you taking foolish risks, Danr Sigurdsson. I'll have wasted my time if you ruin things now.'

'Ruin things? I was on my way to rescue you!' He slid his sword back into its scabbard, his temper rising. 'And you had no right to go there at all! You stole the pendants!'

'I know, but we can argue about that later. As you can see, I didn't need rescuing. Here.' She shoved the leather pouch into his hands. 'You can have them back now anyway. I'm finished with them.'

'You're *finished with them*?'

'Hush!' She reached up and clamped a hand over his mouth. 'He won't need to track us with all the noise you're making. I said we can argue later.'

Danr fumed inwardly as she walked on again, his jaw tingling in the place where her fingers had just touched him, wanting to rant, but unable to deny the truth of her words either. He satisfied himself with a few muttered oaths, then followed grudgingly as they waded across the river and started to climb upwards.

'Do I have permission to speak yet?' He found his voice again when they turned to come back down the hillside, glaring at the back of her head.

'If you must.'

'Yes, I must. What do you think you were playing at, going there?' He reached for her arm, spinning her round to face him. 'I don't understand. *You're* the one who talks about being safe in the forest and not wanting to be around people. Then you go and do something like this! You put yourself in danger! Why?'

Her gaze faltered for a moment. 'I told you, I want to help you get justice for your family.'

'I *said* I didn't want any help.'

'I know, but it was a good idea.'

'It was a damned good idea, but I told you not to go. You could have been hurt.'

'But I wasn't.' She wrested her arm free. 'Knut values my skills too much to let any harm come to me.'

'Knut's not the one you need to worry about. Joarr might have other ideas.' He reached for her hand this time, needing to touch her, to assure himself that she was all right. 'I was worried! If anything had happened to you I'd never have forgiven myself.'

'I'm sorry.' Her expression wavered. 'I hoped I'd be back before you woke up. I shouldn't have stolen your pouch, but it was necessary.'

'No, it wasn't! You were just lucky I slept longer than usual this morning, or I might have charged into the village after you and— Wait!' He stopped mid-sentence. 'That's *why* you gave me the mead, wasn't it? You *wanted* me to sleep longer! You planned this!'

'Yes.' She lifted her chin, her expression unrepentant.

'You gave me that mead just so I would sleep! You *tricked* me?'

'Not exactly. It's not as if I poured it down your throat.'

'It was still a trick.' He ground the words out from between clenched teeth. Whether or not she'd forced him to drink anything, she'd done it with an ulterior motive. She'd done it to deceive him. It didn't matter that she'd done it to help him. Just like at the massacre, he'd been tricked by a woman. Only this time it was a woman he'd trusted—a woman he loved. The betrayal felt ten times worse.

'I'll see you back at the roundhouse.'

'Why? Where are you going?'

'To make sure you're not being followed!' He shot her a savage look as she opened her mouth to object. 'Not another word! I'm starting to think I preferred it when you *didn't* talk. You do things your way. I'll do them mine.'

* * *

Sissa heaved a sigh as Danr stormed away. It was a shame he'd woken up before she'd got back, but it couldn't be helped. At least she'd done what she'd set out to do. She'd found out something important, something he'd want to know if he ever calmed down enough to come back and listen.

The extent of his anger had surprised her. She'd expected *some*, but she'd also expected him to calm down once he saw she was safe. She'd actually thought he might be *glad* she'd gone in his place, but he hadn't even asked whether she'd seen Hilda, let alone shown her the pendants. Oddly enough, he seemed angrier about her giving him the mead than at her taking them, but it wasn't as if she'd added a sleeping draught to his cup—although the thought *had* crossed her mind. All she'd done was make sure he'd had enough mead to ensure a heavy night's sleep. *Tricked* seemed an excessive accusation.

She clicked her tongue for Tove. Halvar, as usual, had chosen to accompany Danr, which was probably a good thing under the circumstances. If Danr was too angry to be alert to potential dangers, then at least the wolf would notice them for him. Halvar would protect him, too, if it came to it, although she hoped it wouldn't. She was probably imagining dangers that weren't real anyway. Despite the granite look on Joarr's face when she'd left, it had seemed to her unlikely that he would defy his kinsman, especially when he was living as a guest in his hall.

She made her way back to the roundhouse and

scooped out some leftover stew from the pot over the fire pit. It tasted slightly burnt, but it was better than nothing. She ate a few mouthfuls, then fetched a needle and thread, trying to focus her attention on sewing. It was impossible. She stabbed her finger half-a-dozen times in the first minute before giving up. Maybe, after all, she *had* been in the wrong—about the mead anyway. Maybe she *had* gone too far and it had been an unfair trick, but her intentions had been good ones. She certainly hadn't meant any harm. Not like— She pinched her lips and closed her eyes at the thought. Not like the woman who'd tricked him before, the one who'd lured him away while his family were slaughtered...

She stood up at the sound of footsteps, just in time to see Danr emerge from the trees, his expression still as furious as before.

'You tricked me.' He stopped on the other side of the fire pit, levelling an accusatory glare at her.

'Yes.' She didn't try to deny it this time.

'You tricked me so that you could go against my wishes. Despite everything I said!'

'Yes.' She took a step forward. 'It reminded you of her, didn't it? The woman who seduced you?'

His lip curled. 'I never thought I'd say this about you, but, yes, it reminded me of her.'

'Then I'm sorry, but it was the opposite really. I was trying to help, not hurt you.'

'And what if something had happened to you? Don't you think *that* would have hurt me?'

'I...' She hesitated. 'I didn't think of it like that.'

'No, because you're determined to do everything on your own, aren't you, Sissa? To live on your own, act on your own…'

'What if I am? I make my own decisions!' She could feel her own temper starting to rise. 'You're not my mate! You've no right to tell me what I can and can't do.'

'I do when the matter concerns me!'

'Not necessarily. I let you stay on condition that you followed *my* rules, remember?'

'Well, maybe it's time for things to change.'

'*I* decide if things change.' She clenched her fists.

'No, trust works both ways, Sissa, and you just betrayed mine.'

'Only because I was trying to protect you. I didn't want you to fight!'

'Sometimes it's the only way.'

'But I didn't want you to be hurt. I didn't want to—'

'What?' His gaze sharpened as she bit her lip. 'You didn't want to what?'

'Nothing.' She turned her face away. 'And aren't you ever going to ask me what I found out about the pendants?'

'You found something out?' He tensed immediately.

'Yes. I did.'

'What?'

'Maybe I don't want to tell you.' She folded her arms pointedly across her chest. 'Especially if you're determined to keep shouting at me.'

'I'm not shouting.'

'It sounds like shouting.'

'Everything sounds like shouting to a woman who hasn't spoken in five years!'

'It's *still* shouting!'

'Fine.' A muscle clenched in his jaw. 'Then I apologise for shouting.'

'*And* for being ungrateful.'

'I'm not—'

'Seeing as my plan worked.'

'I'll admit I overreacted, if you promise not to go anywhere near Joarr again.'

'I've no intention of going near him. Why would I?'

'*And* that you never trick me like that again, not for any reason.'

'I already told you, it wasn't like that. I was *trying* to help you.'

'That's it!' He took three long strides and closed his arms around her.

'What are y—?' She didn't finish the question, her voice muffled as he covered her mouth with his own. Instinctively, she jerked backwards, but he clasped a hand around the back of her neck, holding her in place as he kissed her with a hard, ardent fervour. For a moment she didn't respond, too surprised to do anything, then she opened her lips and let his tongue slip inside. It felt good to feel his mouth against hers again, to feel the warmth of his body through his tunic, too, inviting her to press even closer... She leaned into him, spreading her hands over his shoulder blades while his other hand slid over her lower back, pressing her tight against him.

But they were arguing, weren't they? a voice in the

back of her head reminded her. He'd already made her care too much about him and now he was trying to tell her what she could and couldn't do...

'No!' She moved her hands to his chest, pushing him away. 'I was content before you came along! I was surviving. You can't just come here and refuse to leave and talk too much and...*steal my wolf*!' She flung an arm out towards Halvar. 'You can't say you've made some kind of vow about women and *still* kiss me! You can't tell me how to live either!'

'I know. I'm sorry. I didn't mean—'

'You need to go.' She balled her hands into fists. 'I found out what you wanted. Hilda's innocent.'

'What?'

'She didn't have anything to do with your massacre, I'm sure of it. So you don't have to fight anyone. You can just go and ask your questions and then leave.'

His face hardened again. 'I'm not going anywhere.'

'What?'

'I'm not leaving you here on your own. It's not safe. You need protection.'

'I've managed perfectly well on my own for years!'

'That doesn't mean you're indestructible. Even aside from the weather, it only takes one man to *not* be frightened of you, to come and find you...'

'To get past Tove and Halvar?'

'Even wolves can't fight swords. And they don't live for ever either. You're too vulnerable here.'

'That's my choice!' She glared at him angrily. Asking her if he could stay was one thing—telling her was something else entirely! 'I never agreed that you could come back here, let alone stay. And what about your oath? You said it was more important to you than your own life. How are you going to fulfil it if you don't get the answers you came for?'

'I don't know.' He pushed his hands through his hair. 'All I know is that you're more important now. More than my oath, more than my life even. Sissa...' He reached for her again. 'I can't stand the thought of anything happening to you. I was terrified today. I love you.'

She jumped away from him, feeling a cold sweat break out on her neck. The words ought to have been precious. Once upon a time they were ones she'd longed to hear, but that girl was long gone and all she could feel now was a rising tide of panic. He loved her and she loved him, only she hadn't let herself acknowledge it until now. That was the real reason she'd gone to the village, because she'd been so scared of losing him, another person she loved.

I didn't want to lose you. Those were the words she'd been going to say before, but it was all too much, too quickly. She wasn't ready to hear him say he loved her—or to think it herself yet. But it was too late to unthink it and the realisation was terrifying. Despite all her efforts to protect her heart, he'd already found a place there. It made her even more vulnerable than he'd just said and she couldn't bear the thought of being vulnerable again. Which meant that her only option was to send him away and tell him not to come back—not when his oath was fulfilled, not ever. She had to get her life back to the way it had been before he'd arrived and become invulnerable again.

'Sissa…' He was still looking at her. 'Did you hear what I said? I love you.'

'Kolga.' She swallowed, amazed by how calm her voice sounded when she felt as if she'd just been shaken to her core.

'What?' He stared at her, his expression frozen.

'I heard your stepmother whisper it to Joarr when she saw the pendants. Who's Kolga?'

Chapter Eighteen

'Kolga is the name of Hilda's sister, but what does she have to do with anything?'

'I don't know, but that's what I heard.' Sissa dug her teeth into her bottom lip, apparently unable to meet his gaze any longer.

'Kolga…' Danr drew his brows together, wondering how they'd gone from his declaration of love to the name of his step-aunt in just a few short heartbeats. It was the first time in his life he'd said the words *I love you*, but either she hadn't heard or she was choosing to ignore them. From the horrified expression on her face, it was obviously the latter. So much for taking a second chance on happiness together. She looked as if she were about to be sick.

As for Kolga…she'd always hated his father, but there had never been any evidence linking her to the massacre. Until now.

'Maybe you came after the wrong woman?' Sissa

said the words quietly, moving away to the other side of the fire pit.

'Or maybe she and Hilda planned the massacre together?'

'No. I saw her face. I didn't see any guilt there.'

'You don't know her the way I do.'

'I'm not determined to find her guilty either.' She pursed her lips. 'Now you can take a branch of peace and go and speak to her calmly. Just make sure Knut is there to watch Joarr.'

He gritted his teeth. 'Are you trying to get rid of me now?'

For a moment her expression wavered and then went blank. It was the old impassive expression she'd been wearing the first time he saw her, as if she were retreating inside herself before his very eyes. 'Yes. You came here for a reason, remember? You'll never be able to carry on with your life otherwise.'

'What about us?' He was already bracing himself for the worst. 'What about the fact that I just told you I loved you?'

'I never asked for your love. I told you from the start, I live alone. That means for ever. Now you need to go and fulfil your oath.' She hesitated briefly. 'Leave me in peace, Norseman. I don't want you to come back.'

Sissa bumped the cauldron painfully against her leg as she marched towards the river. She didn't particularly want any water—it was starting to rain again anyhow—but she needed to put some distance between her and Danr. She'd told him to leave, which meant that she had to keep away until he'd gone so she wouldn't be tempted to change her mind.

She glanced over her shoulder, making sure he hadn't decided to follow her. He hadn't. Neither had Tove nor Halvar this time either, the pair of them slinking off into the forest when she and Danr had started to argue. No doubt Tove would come and find her soon enough, but Halvar would probably still stay with his new favourite.

She flung herself down by the riverbank, pressing a hand to her stinging eyes. She'd spoken impulsively when she'd told him to leave, but she'd made the right decision for both of them. She should never have even considered letting him share her life. She was safer and better off on her own. Now it was too late to deny that she loved him, but she *could* stop herself from caring any more than she already did. She could barricade her heart and try to forget the expression on his face when she'd said that she'd never asked for his love. She could even force herself to feel anger again, too. How *dared* he try to tell her how to live and insist that he stay to protect her! She didn't need him or anyone. She was in control of her own life and the sooner he was out of it, the better. In a month or so, he'd be nothing more than a handsome memory.

Even though she was quite certain her heart would break anyway.

A twig cracked behind her and she spun around, the hairs on the back of her neck prickling with awareness. There was no sign of anyone or anything, but there was a new feeling of tension in the air. She had the distinct impression of being watched—hunted—and not by Danr. It was someone else… She reached a hand out for her spear and realised she'd left it behind when she'd run away. She was alone, weaponless and wolf-less…

Slowly, she reached for the cauldron handle—at least she could use that as a weapon if she had to— and braced her knees, getting ready to run when another twig cracked from a different direction and a hand wound its way around her throat, closely followed by another over her mouth. Instinctively, she kicked backwards, swinging the cauldron behind her, pleased to hear a grunt of pain as it connected with something, then she was falling and whoever was holding her was falling, too, and then…she was aware of a thud, a shooting pain in her skull, followed by darkness.

Women! Danr rammed his few belongings into a pack. No, not women—*woman*! There was only one woman in the world who had this much power over him, the power to make him feel angry and infatuated and distraught all at the same time, as if he were going crazy! It was ironic really. For the first time in his life, here he was trying to do the right thing by a woman, to help and protect and *love* her, and she'd thrown it back in his face. Why couldn't she see that?

On the other hand, he wasn't exactly blameless. He'd handled the whole situation badly. He shouldn't just have announced that he was staying, or said that she needed his protection either. She'd been the capable one from the start—the one who'd rescued him—and his words *had* broken the rules of their arrangement.

Maybe he ought to go and find her and apologise.
Maybe he ought to grovel again. Maybe he ought to
kiss her until she saw sense… No. He shook his head
before his imagination got carried away. Kissing her
would only make a bad situation even worse, just as it
had before. Only, he hadn't been able to *not* kiss her
then. He'd wanted to hold her tight in his arms because
he'd been so relieved that she was all right and because
she was beautiful and infuriating and brave and everything he'd ever wanted in a woman.

But she didn't want him. She'd told him to go and
never come back.

He stood and slung the pack over his shoulder. In
that case, it was probably best for him to leave without saying goodbye. *I don't want you to come back.*
The words made his jaw clench. For a little while, he'd
thought it might be possible for them to seize a second
chance together, but maybe he didn't deserve another
chance, after all. Maybe losing the woman he loved
and being alone was his real punishment. It certainly
felt like one. After all his years of avoiding love and
the pain and regret that went with it, he'd fallen into
the same trap as his mother after all…

He ran a hand over Halvar's head, murmuring a
few words of farewell, before looking around for Tove.
She was stalking up and down the clearing, making
low whining sounds, which was…odd. The wolf was
usually Sissa's shadow, but now she seemed anxious.

'She's probably just gone for a walk to calm down,'
he called across to the wolf, trying to reassure them
both. 'No need to worry.'

But he ought to go and make sure, he decided. The last time he'd seen her she'd been heading towards the gorge, a cauldron in her hand, obviously wanting to get away from him. She wouldn't appreciate him going after her, but now the tingle of foreboding at the back of his mind wouldn't let him leave without seeing her. He started in that direction, his footsteps picking up speed as he went, though they still didn't seem quick enough. It felt like the day before all over again and yet somehow even worse. It was *his* fault that she'd stormed away this time. If he hadn't argued, hadn't threatened not to leave, hadn't told her he loved her...

At last he emerged out of the trees, his heart stalling at the sight of the cauldron lying on its side by the riverbank.

'Joarr.' He ground out the name, the sight of two sets of footprints in the mud telling him everything he needed to know. In one spot in particular they were all muddled together and overlapping, as if there had been some kind of struggle.

He dropped his pack and ran back to the clearing.

Chapter Nineteen

There were raised voices around her. Sissa became aware of them gradually as she rose back to consciousness. By the feel of it she was lying, tied up, on some kind of bed, but she didn't move, listening to the argument going on around her. Tempted as she was to open her eyes and watch, too, she suspected the voices would stop the moment she did. Not that it overly mattered since she recognised them anyway. They belonged to Knut, Joarr, Alva and Hilda, all of them in varying degrees of anger or distress.

'You shouldn't have done this!' Knut sounded angriest of all.

'She had the pendants.' Joarr's response was terse. 'That means she's seen him and she probably knows where he is.'

'You thought he was dead a day ago. Maybe she only found his body.'

'He's alive, I know it. Why would she have come

here and accused Hilda unless he'd sent her? Trust Danr to find the only woman in an entire forest!'

'I don't know why she came, but you still shouldn't have attacked her.'

'Knut's right.' It was Hilda's voice this time. 'You said you were going to look for Danr, not her.'

'I found her first. She was alone and it was too good an opportunity to lose, but I didn't attack her. I was only going to gag her mouth and tie her hands, but she wouldn't stop struggling. She knocked us both over. That's how she hit her head.'

Sissa winced. At least that explained the sore feeling on the back of her skull. Obviously Joarr had brought her back to the village, but how long had she been unconscious? How long had it been since her argument with Danr? Would he have guessed what had happened by now? And if he had, would he come after her?

She almost moaned aloud at the thought. Of course he would come. He'd been about to come here with a branch of peace anyway, only now she had a horrible feeling that he wouldn't be feeling quite so peaceful...

'This isn't my fight.' Knut's tone was grave. 'I want no part of it.'

'You don't have to be part of it. He'll come. Danr's many things, but he's no coward.'

'And then what?'

'Then we fight properly. To the death this time.'

'No!' Hilda's voice rose higher in protest.

'Yes. You said he was convinced that you had some part in the massacre and that your sons thought so, too. That means he came here for revenge. I won't let him hurt you.'

'If I could just go and speak to my sons face to face…'

'Sandulf *knew* he was coming.'

'But if you kill him…' her voice cracked '…they'll never believe that I'm innocent. They'll never forgive me either. There has to be another way.'

'There isn't.'

'My lord?' A new voice spoke up. 'There's a warrior outside the gates. He looks Norse.'

'Good.' Joarr sounded pleased. 'He's here even sooner than I expected.'

Sissa tensed, waiting a few moments until the sound of hurried footsteps had receded before opening her eyes and wriggling up into a sitting position. She couldn't just stay there. She had to free herself so she could stop Joarr and Danr from killing each other. Her hands and feet were bound, but perhaps if she… She blinked, suddenly aware that she wasn't alone in the chamber. Hilda was sitting on a stool beside the bed, clearly as surprised to see her awake as she was to be seen.

'You're awake!' After a moment's hesitation, Hilda shot out of her seat and made for the door.

'Wait!' Sissa called out impulsively. Given time she might have thought of some other way to communicate without revealing her secret, but she didn't have time…

'You can speak?' Hilda stopped and swivelled around, doubly surprised now. 'They said that you couldn't.'

'I know.' Sissa rolled her legs over the side of the bed with an effort. 'But we *need* to talk—and we need to hurry.'

'I should summon Knut…' Hilda glanced towards the doorway uncertainly.

'Why? He's not the one who wants to kill Danr. That's Joarr, but you don't want them to fight either, do you?'

'No.' Hilda put her hands over her cheeks and shook her head. 'Joarr thinks he can win, but Danr's a fearsome warrior even with an injured arm and I *know* he spared him the last time. I saw him hesitate. He won't do that again, especially if he's come to rescue you.'

'Danr spared Joarr?' Sissa felt her spirits lift. He hadn't told her that.

'Yes. There was a moment when he could have killed him, but he didn't. He didn't want to. I could see it in his eyes.' Hilda paused and frowned. 'Danr hates me, but he and Joarr were close once.'

'Good. Now tell me the truth and quickly. *Did* you order your husband's murder?'

'What? No!' Even from the across the room, Sissa could see the blaze of anger in the other woman's eyes. 'A hundred times, no!'

'I didn't think so.' Sissa lifted her legs and jerked her head towards them. 'Now untie me and we can stop them from killing each other.'

'How?'

'Let me speak to Danr. I'll tell him you're innocent. He was halfway to believing it already. He was getting ready to come here under a branch of peace.'

'He was?' Hilda blinked. 'But what does that matter now? After what Joarr's done to you, he won't care. He'll fight just to avenge the insult.'

'I'll convince him there's no need for bloodshed.'

'I don't think so.' Hilda's expression turned faintly pitying. 'I've known Danr all his life. He's good at convincing women to do things for him, but just because he's seduced you doesn't mean that he cares or that he'll listen to you. He's only been using you like all the rest of his women.'

'You're wrong.' Sissa lifted her feet higher impatiently. 'He's not the man he used to be and I'm nothing like *the rest of his women.* I know he'll listen. Now, untie me. It's the only way.'

'How do I know this isn't a trick?' Hilda took a few cautious steps forward. 'They told me you're dangerous.'

'They also told you I couldn't talk. Do I *look* dangerous to you?'

'Not at the moment.'

'Exactly! Look, my name's Sissa, I've absolutely no power over the weather and we're wasting time and energy. Somebody could be dead by the time you decide what to do.'

'Do you promise not to hurt me?'

'Only if you hurry.'

'All right.' Hilda crouched down and pulled at the bindings. 'But I know Danr and he won't listen.'

'I know Danr better and he *will.*' Sissa stood up and flexed her muscles. 'Or I'll fight him myself.'

* * *

Danr walked undisturbed through the open gates of the village. After donning his mail and weapons he'd stood for a few moments with Tove and Halvar beside the fire pit, reining in the feelings of dread and anger and trying to think clearly. The time when he might have gone to the village under a branch of peace had passed. Joarr's actions weren't those of a man who wanted peace. They were a deliberate insult, a declaration of war. They left him no option about what to do next. It wouldn't get him the answers he'd come for or fulfil his oath either, but at that moment he didn't care. All he cared about was rescuing Sissa and returning her back to the forest again.

He found Joarr standing outside the great hall as he approached, sword already in hand. A red-haired and stern-looking man, most likely his kinsman Knut, stood beside him, while warriors were lined up around the walls of the surrounding buildings, though their weapons were all sheathed. At least the fight would be honourable then...

'How's the arm?' Joarr called out when he saw him.

Danr didn't answer, coming to a halt a few feet away instead. 'Do you have her?'

'Your woman? I do.'

'She's not *my* woman. She's her own. And if you've laid as much as a finger on her...'

'I haven't.'

'Good.' Danr drew his own sword from its scabbard, holding it in front of his face despite the spasm of pain that immediately shot up his arm. 'Because she has nothing to do with any of this.'

'You involved her when you sent her here with those pendants.'

'I didn't send her.' He clenched his jaw at the accusation. 'I didn't know she was coming.'

'Then why did she?'

'To help me.' Danr tipped his sword sideways, laying it across both of his hands before tossing it into the dirt at Joarr's feet. 'Now let her go and you can take me as your prisoner instead.'

'What is this?' Joarr glanced down at the sword and then back up again. 'Some kind of trick?'

'No trick.'

'You'd exchange places with her? What if I intend to kill you? Are you really prepared to die for a woman?'

'Yes.' He didn't hesitate. 'She's innocent in all of this. Just like Ingrid and Gilla were. Enough innocent blood has been spilled. So let her go and kill me if you have to.'

Joarr lowered his blade halfway to the ground. 'I don't want to kill you, Danr, but Hilda's innocent, too. If you can't accept that, then we need to end this once and for all. Either you leave Skíð or we fight, to the death this time.'

'I'm not going anywhere until I find out the truth about those pendants. They belonged to Hilda and they were used to pay the assassins.' Danr lifted an eyebrow. 'Doesn't that seem suspicious to you?'

'I don't care what it seems. I know what I know.'

'I only want to talk to her.'

'Do you really expect me to trust you?' Joarr took a threatening step forward. 'The last time I saw you, you had a sword to her throat!'

'That was a mistake. I thought I could provoke her into admitting her guilt, that's all.'

Joarr's brow creased before he kicked the sword back through the dirt towards him. 'You were always a wily one, boy, but I won't let you within ten feet of her. I'll let your woman go, but only on condition that *we* fight.'

'If that's what you want.' Danr reached down, taking hold of his sword again. 'But I don't want to kill you either, Joarr. How many times have we fought side by side? You were like a father to me once.' He felt the old rush of resentment. 'Before *her.*'

'I know.' For a moment Joarr's voice betrayed a hint of sadness. 'But that was a long time ago now.'

They stared at each other for a few seconds, both of them sombre, before Joarr lunged, thrusting his sword out like a spear. Danr twisted away quickly, lifting Bitterblade to parry the blow and twist it sideways, then using both of his hands on his sword to push Joarr and his weapon backwards. With his weakened arm, he wouldn't be able to fight for long. He still didn't want to kill Joarr, but if he could just incapacitate him...

'Stop!'

They both froze, their weapons suspended in mid-air as Hilda's voice rang through the village. Except it wasn't just Hilda's voice, Danr realised. It was Sissa's, too.

He exchanged a swift look with Joarr and then

turned his head to see the women standing side by side outside the hall.

'Don't interfere.' Joarr's voice was a growl. 'This is between me and him.'

'No, it's not.' Hilda's voice was as imperious as Danr remembered it. 'It's between all of us and there won't be any more fighting between the two of you, not today, not ever.'

'Sissa? Are you all right?' Danr started forward, but Joarr's raised sword held him back.

'Yes, but you need to put your sword down, too, Danr. There's no need for fighting.'

'You can speak?' Knut looked stunned.

'She can and she's very persuasive, too.' To Danr's amazement, Hilda reached for Sissa's hand, clasping it in hers before glaring at him and Joarr. 'And if the two of you want either of us to as much as acknowledge your existences ever again, you can stop being so foolish and *male* and come inside. We have a lot to talk about.'

Chapter Twenty

'What's going on? What is this?' Danr glared across the hearth to where Sissa stood calmly beside Hilda. As relieved as he'd been to find her unharmed, the sight of her clasping hands with his old enemy made him livid.

'Patience, Danr.' Hilda fixed him with a look, as if she knew exactly what thoughts were going through his mind. 'We're going to talk properly, the way we should have done that first day on the beach.'

'As I recall, you told me to go away.'

'I'm not saying I was blameless, but you caught me by surprise,' she retorted, her chin inching higher. 'We've always loathed each other, Danr, I won't deny that, but Sissa says you came to Skíð to ask questions, *not* to kill me. Is that true?'

'Yes.' He controlled the impulse to argue just for the sake of it. 'I came only to ask about the arrow pendants. Rurik and Sandulf found them among the assassins' belongings. Sandulf would have come and asked you about them himself, but he had to take two children

to Eireann so I offered to come instead. I swear I had
no intention of killing you that day.'

'You looked convincing to me,' Joarr growled.

'I know, but it was an act. I only wanted to scare
her.'

'Then you did a very good job.' Hilda pursed her
lips. 'Although if you *really* thought I was involved in
the massacre then I suppose I can understand why.'

'Hild—'

She lifted a hand to quiet Joarr. 'On my life, I swear
I had nothing to do with it. I would never have endan-
gered my sons, let alone Ingrid and Gilla. I loved them.'

'I know that now.' Danr threw a quick glance towards Sissa. 'But at the time, I suppose I wanted you
to be guilty. I wanted to hear you confess.'

'Understandable.' She sounded unsurprised. 'I
would probably have blamed you, too, if I could have.
I suppose you wanted to be the one to punish me as
well?'

'No.' He shook his head. 'I would have taken you
to your sons and let them do it. I promised Sandulf I
wouldn't hurt you no matter what I discovered.'

'So Sandulf really believes I might have been involved?' A pained expression crossed her face.

'I wouldn't say that.' Was he trying to make her feel
better now? 'I don't think he truly believes it, but he
recognised the pendants as yours. He—*we* only want
to know how the assassins came by them.'

'I've been wondering the same thing.' Her brow
knitted. 'After you mentioned them, I convinced myself
you must have been talking about different pendants,

but then when Sissa showed them to me… It made me sick to think that anything of mine was used to pay for the murder of Ingrid and Gilla. It didn't make any sense. It still doesn't.'

'Then you don't know why the assassins had them?'

'Not exactly…'

'What does *that* mean?' He frowned. 'Either you know or you don't.'

'Then I don't. It can't be what it looks like.'

'What does it look like?' He resisted the urge to walk across the hall and shake her. 'Sissa said you whispered something about Kolga when she showed them to you.'

'Ye-es.' For a moment Hilda looked on the verge of saying something else before twisting her face away.

'She said she gave them to Kolga after an argument with Sigurd,' Joarr answered for her. 'She said she couldn't bear the sight of them any longer.'

'That wasn't exactly the whole truth.' Hilda's voice sounded pained. 'That is, I did give them to her, but not because of an argument. The truth is, I *had* to give them to her. She threatened to tell Sigurd about us.'

'She was blackmailing you?' Joarr's expression turned ferocious. 'Why didn't you tell me?'

'Because I thought it was better to deal with it myself. And it wasn't blackmail—not exactly. It was… an arrangement.'

'It sounds like blackmail to me.'

'And me.' Danr folded his arms.

'Oh, *now* the pair of you find something to agree on!' Hilda threw her arms up. 'Whatever it was, I don't understand how they could have ended up with the assassins.'

'What did your sister think of your husband?' Sissa asked quietly.

'She liked him herself at first.' Hilda shifted uncomfortably. 'She was jealous when I married him, but that was years ago.'

'Was she bitter?'

'Perhaps a little—especially because of the way he used to mock Eithr, her son—but I still can't believe she would have ordered the massacre. Why would she?'

'Because she was always a cold-hearted bitch,' Joarr spoke gruffly.

'Something else we agree on.' Danr nodded wholeheartedly. 'I loathed *her* even more than I loathed you—no offence—but if she used the pendants to pay the assassins then she must have known they would be traced back to you.'

'Which means that she framed you.' Joarr looked ferocious again.

'No!' Hilda shook her head adamantly. 'She's my sister. We had our differences, but she wouldn't have done that. And even if she *did* hate Sigurd, why would she have killed all the others? Why Ingrid and Gilla? She had no quarrel with them.'

'Maybe not, but you have to admit that she's profited by Brandt losing the kingdom. It went to her son.'

'But Thorfinn acts as his guardian. Eithr's far too weak to rule on his own.' Hilda snapped her fingers. '*Thorfinn!* He could have been the one behind it.'

Danr threw a questioning look at Joarr. 'He would

have had access to the pendants if they were in her possession. It's possible. Either way I need to tell Brandt.'

'Brandt?' Hilda's voice softened immediately. 'Where is he?'

'The last I heard he was in Eireann with Alarr. They're both well. Alarr and Sandulf are married now, too.'

'Married?'

'So is Rurik…' he gave her a pointed look '…if you're interested.'

As he'd expected, her eyes flashed instantly. 'Why would I be interested in Rurik?'

'Maybe after fourteen years of living in the same hall?'

'He still has nothing to do with me.'

'Oh, stop it.' Sissa glared at them both in turn. 'Stop goading each other. This has gone on long enough. You—' she gestured at Danr '—you almost got yourself killed because of this feud and you—' she waved her other arm at Hilda '—you almost got your husband killed! How many years have you spent being resentful and jealous of each other? And all over a man who sounds as though he didn't deserve either of you! So either fight it out yourselves or stop talking altogether, but leave the rest of us out of it.'

'She makes a good point.' Joarr rubbed a hand around the back of his neck.

'She does not.' Hilda lifted her chin in the air stubbornly. 'I've never been jealous of *him*.'

'If you weren't then you wouldn't be so determined to argue. Now, neither of you is leaving this hall until you resolve it.' Sissa jerked her head towards the others. 'Come on. I want some air.'

'I've never heard anything so vile.' Hilda glared at him. 'As if I'd be jealous of you!'

'Well, maybe not me exactly, but since my mother isn't around to be jealous of...' Danr sighed. 'Maybe Sissa's right. You know, for a woman who's spent so many years living without people, she understands a lot about them. I was always jealous of Brandt and Alarr and Sandulf because they belonged in Father's hall. Maybe I was jealous of you, too.'

'What do you mean?' Hilda's chin lowered infinitesimally. 'Sigurd acknowledged you.'

'But I was still a bastard. I never felt...necessary, not when he had three legitimate sons. Good, strong, clever sons. I spent years trying to get his attention.'

'You had it. He was always boasting about you and your exploits.'

'Don't remind me.' Danr made a face. 'I'm not proud of the way I behaved, but my exploits, as you call them, always seemed to amuse him.'

'No doubt they reminded him of his time with your mother.'

'My mother was a good woman.' He felt a fresh stirring of anger. 'She would never have run away with him if he hadn't lied to her.'

'I know.' Hilda's tone shifted as she sat down on a hearth bench. 'In truth, I felt sorry for her in a way, even though I hated her, too. It wasn't fair of me. It wasn't fair of me to hate you and Rurik either, but...'

'You were unhappy.'

'Yes. I was married to a man I'd come to despise. That was bad enough, but when he brought you to live in *my* household, I was furious. I felt insulted, but I shouldn't have taken it out on you. You were just boys.'

'I probably didn't help.' Danr lowered himself onto the bench beside her. 'I was always baiting you, but you made it so easy.'

'I did no—' She stopped mid-way through her protest. 'All right, maybe I did. I was a hypocrite, too.'

'How so?'

'I was always berating you for your behaviour, but my relationship with Joarr began sooner than it should have.'

'I know.'

'What?'

'Joarr's never been very good at dissembling. You were better at hiding it, but I knew.'

She shifted around to look him full in the face. 'Then why didn't you tell your father? That would *definitely* have got his attention. You could have had your revenge on me, too.'

'I don't know.' He shrugged. 'Maybe by that time I already knew his attention wasn't worth having. Or maybe because Joarr had always been more of a father to me and I didn't want him to suffer. Or maybe I just felt sorry for you.'

'You felt *sorry* for me?' Her chin whipped up indignantly.

'You see?' He grinned. 'Easy.'

She stared at him for a long moment. 'You're not the Danr I remember.'

'I hope not. I don't think any of us are the same after what happened that day in Maerr.'

'It's not just that. You were different afterwards, yes, but today a woman ordered you to put down your sword and talk to your stepmother and you did it. The Danr I remember would never have even considered such a thing. He told women what to do, not the other way around.' Her expression turned quizzical. 'You were truly prepared to die for her, weren't you?'

'It was my fault she was here in the first place.'

'Is that the only reason?'

'No.' He paused. 'She's…different.'

'She's certainly that. They say she lives all alone in the forest.'

'Yes, until I came along. She found me dying and saved my life. Then I convinced her to let me stay.' He made a face as she arched an eyebrow. 'Because of my cooking actually.'

'That's *all*?' Her eyebrow stayed where it was. 'Because it would be easy to take advantage of a woman like that.'

'No, it wouldn't.' He snorted. 'Trust me.'

'So you haven't…?'

'No.'

'*You* haven't?'

'No!'

'I'm impressed… Why not?'

'*Why not?*' He gave an incredulous laugh. 'I thought you of all people would be pleased.'

'I am. I like her. This is the first time I've ever approved of one of your women.'

'I already told Joarr, she isn't my woman.'

'But does she want to be?' Hilda sounded concerned rather than sceptical. 'Because you weren't just good at getting women into bed, Danr. You could make them fall in love with you, too. Maybe not intentionally, but you did. It's what I hated the most about your behaviour. It reminded me so much of your father when he was young. I loved him then.'

'I wish it were the case,' he sighed, 'but it's the other way round. She wants me to leave Skíð and never come back.'

'Ah.'

'Maybe it's for the best and she's better off without a man like me.' He ran a hand over his face. 'I already know I'm not worthy. Maybe you were right and I'm not capable of real love either.'

'I might have said you were shallow, Danr, but I never said you weren't capable of love. You loved your mother. I saw how much it affected you when she died. And you love your brothers, too, I've always known that. *And* your father. You wouldn't have been so desperate for his approval if you hadn't loved him.'

He nodded, aware of a lump in his throat. 'Do you think he ever cared about any of us in return?'

'Sigurd loved Sigurd, but inasmuch as he *could* love, he loved you. He loved all of his sons.'

'Thank you…' he swallowed '…but Sissa still might be better off without me. You said I inherited the worst of him, that I was shallow and soulless.'

'I was angry.'

'But you meant it.'

'At the time, yes.'

'I don't want to be like that. I don't want to be my father.'

To his surprise, she reached across and patted his arm. 'Something tells me you aren't, at least not any more. Maybe you would have been if things had stayed as they were in Maerr, but, much as it pains me to say it, you might have become a better man, after all, Danr.'

'That's the nicest thing you've ever said to me.'

'Don't get used to it.' She gave him an arch look and then glanced towards the door. 'But I wouldn't be so sure that she wants you to leave. When she woke up, all she thought about was saving you. Most women would have been afraid for themselves, but she thought only of you. She probably just saved your life.'

'She does that.' He gave a half-smile. 'It's becoming a habit.'

'Maybe that means she's good for you.' Hilda nudged him in the ribs with her elbow and he laughed.

'If only Father could see us now. I never imagined I'd ever sit and have a conversation with you about love.'

'Neither did I. *Do* you love her, Danr?'

'Yes.'

'Then you should tell her.'

'I did. That's why she told me to leave.'

'Because you told her you loved her?'

He made a face. 'That and because she wants her

life back the way it was before. She wants to be on her own.'

'Completely alone? Why?'

'Her home was destroyed in a raid five years ago. She lost her family and everyone she knew. Now she doesn't want to be around people any more. She doesn't trust them, warriors especially. She says she's safer on her own.'

'But she still helped you? And she still helps the people here, too?'

'Yes. She's a healer. She says it's what she has to do.'

'All right, but then why did she come here with the pendants?'

'To help me.'

'And why did she speak to me earlier? She could have kept silent and nobody would have been any the wiser.'

'Because...' He frowned, aware that he was beginning to repeat himself. 'To help me.'

'Exactly. Even if she doesn't trust people, those aren't the actions of a woman who doesn't care. She wanted to save you more than she wanted to keep away from people.'

'But she still wants me to go.'

'Think about it, Danr. She lost everyone she cared about once. Maybe she's afraid of that happening again? Maybe that's really why she wants to be alone. If she were only afraid of being physically hurt, then wouldn't it make *more* sense to keep a warrior around?'

'So you think she told me to go *because* she cares about me?'

'It's possible.'

'That makes no sense!'

'So many women and so little understanding.' Hilda lifted her eyes skywards. 'It must feel strange to be rejected by a woman for a change.'

'Mmm.' He glared at her. 'It's not a pleasant feeling.'

'No, but it's about time you felt it. Are you really going to give up so easily?'

'I'm respecting her wishes.'

'Then you're a stubborn fool.' Hilda made a scornful sound. 'So what will you do instead?'

'I'll go to Eireann and tell Brandt what I've found out.'

'And then?'

'Then I'll go with him to confront Thorfinn.'

'And after that?'

'Do you *really* care?'

She pursed her lips with a thoughtful expression. 'You know, Joarr's been talking about building a hall of our own, maybe a whole new village. He'll need good men. Warriors.'

Danr sat back and stared at her with disbelief. 'Are you asking me to come back? To live here on the same island as you?'

'I suppose so.' She looked almost as surprised as he was by the idea. 'Maybe I've taken leave of my senses, but I owe you some kind of amends.'

'I must have taken leave of my senses, too...' he shook his head '...because it actually sounds tempting. A new village is a good idea, but I just told you, Sissa doesn't want me back.'

'Maybe she needs time.' Hilda stood up and looked down at him. 'You know, pride was another of your father's weaknesses. He would never have risked being rejected by a woman. Fortunately, you don't want to be like him any more, do you?' She smiled. 'Go and talk to her, Danr. Find out the truth at least. Second chances are hard to come by.'

Chapter Twenty-One

'May I join you?'

Sissa looked around as Knut came towards her. She was standing just outside the hall, close enough to be able to hear raised voices inside if there were any. To her relief, however, there weren't. 'Yes.'

'Your name is Sissa?'

'Yes.'

'You're Norse?'

'Yes.'

'And all this time, all these years, you could talk?'

'Yes.'

'Then why didn't you speak to us?'

He sounded bewildered, though his expression was kind. He would probably have forced Joarr to release her, she thought, if Danr hadn't got there first. And now that he knew she *could* speak, she might as well tell him the truth.

'Because I come from the other side of the island, from the burnt village.'

'But that was destroyed years ago, before we came here.'

'Yes. I was the only survivor.'

'Moon's eye.' He rubbed a hand over his jaw. 'I'm sorry. If I'd known…'

'I didn't want to be near people, warriors especially.'

He nodded as if that made sense. 'Those outlaws struck in several places. Half-a-dozen villages on the islands were destroyed before they were hunted down and captured.'

'They were captured?' She felt as though her heart had just stopped for a moment.

'And punished.' He nodded sombrely. 'Nothing like that has happened since.'

'Good.' She swallowed. 'I'm glad.'

'I'm sorry for what happened, but I promise that no one here will ever harm you or let harm come to you again. If you wish to stay and be our healer, we'll give you a house. You'll be respected and looked after.'

'No.' She shook her head. 'I live alone. Nothing has to change.'

'I understand if that's what you wish.'

There was a heavy silence before Knut turned his head, a look of relief crossing his face at the sight of Danr emerging from the hall. 'So what now for you, Danr Sigurdsson?'

'Now I need to go to Eireann. I need to tell my brothers what I've discovered.'

'So late in the year? The crossing will be rough.'

'It's not so far, but even if it were I'd still have to risk it. Brandt needs to know about Kolga and Thorfinn.'

'Then I'll lend you a boat and some of my men will accompany you.' Knut looked awkwardly between them. 'I'll go and make preparations now.'

'Thank you.' Danr waited until he'd gone before turning towards her, his brow creased with concern. 'Are you sure you're all right after what happened? You weren't mistreated in any way?'

'No. I hit my head and I was bound, but I'm not injured.'

His gaze hardened. 'None of that should have happened. I'm sorry for involving you in all this.'

'You didn't. It was my choice to involve myself.'

'I'm still not happy about it, but I'm grateful. For all of it. And all those things I said before, about not leaving… I shouldn't have. I overreacted. If you want to live in the forest alone, then that's your choice, not mine. I've no right to tell you how to live or to demand to stay. My only excuse is that I was frightened of losing you.' He twisted his face to one side, a muscle tightening in his jaw. 'I've never been so frightened in my life, but then I've never felt this way about anyone before. I never wanted to. I always thought that love led to pain, but now I think I was just waiting for the right woman to come along and find me bleeding to death in the wilderness.' He gave a half-smile. 'But I do understand what you meant about safety being important. When I thought Joarr might hurt you… I never want to feel that way again.

'It's safer not to love, not to risk being hurt. Maybe that's what I've been doing with women my whole life, but that's not the way I want to live any more. I want to be with you, to share my life with you, to make the most of every moment together. I'm not saying you can't manage on your own, just that you don't have to. I'm saying that I want to help to look after you, too. There must be a few things I'm good for and whatever they are, whatever you want, I'll do them. Because I love you, Sissa. I've never said those words to any other woman in my life, but I mean them. I love everything about you. Your strength, your courage, your wild hair. When I'm with you I feel right, like I'm where I'm supposed to be. If you still want me to go, then I'll go, but if you let me come back then I swear I'll be as faithful and loyal as Halvar. I'll probably still talk too much, but I'll make up for it in other ways.' He paused for breath finally. 'What do you think, could you bear to live with a man who loves you? And cooks?'

She opened her mouth and then closed it again. Could she bear all of that? *Yes*. More than that, she wanted it. It all sounded so perfect, but that made it even more dangerous…

'Sissa…' He frowned when she didn't answer. 'You told me once that you survived for your mother, because it's what *she* would have wanted, but wouldn't she have wanted you to be happy and loved, too? Just give me a chance. That's all I ask.'

She tensed as an image of her mother's face flashed into her mind. After all these years, the emotions it evoked were bittersweet. There was sadness, yes, but there was also love and, in the end, that was the strongest feeling of all. Losing her parents would have been easier if she hadn't loved them, but then she would have missed one of the greatest feelings in life. Without that love—the memory of it—she wouldn't have survived. It was the reason she'd survived, but it was Danr who'd brought her back to life again. And if she let him go, then the rest of her life would just be about survival. He was right; that wasn't the life her mother would have wanted for her.

'I always did talk too much.' He inclined his head when she still didn't answer. 'Goodbye, Sissa.'

'Wait.' She put her hand on his arm as he started to turn away. Despite all of her fears, he was right—and she couldn't let him go. 'I overreacted, too. I was scared of caring for you because I was frightened of losing you the way I lost everyone else I cared about, but isn't that foolish, to send a person away *because* you're afraid of losing them? I'd lose you anyway.'

'It sounds foolish to me.' His eyes flickered with hope as he took a cautious step back towards her.

'And I can't go back to the way I lived before anyway. People know I can talk now. Things can't ever be the same any more.'

'I'm sorry.'

'I'm not.' She slid her hand down his arm until her fingers met his. 'I'm *glad*. I'm glad I found you bleeding in the wilderness, Danr Sigurdsson. I'm glad you wouldn't let me send you away. I'm glad because...' She stopped and bit her lip. She still couldn't say that she loved him, not yet, but she could say the next best thing. 'Because I want you to come back. Once you've fulfilled your oath, I want you to come back and be my mate.' She smiled as he clasped both of her hands, lifting them to his lips and covering them in kisses.

'Anything you want. Only marry me first.'

'What?'

'Marry me. Be my mate in truth. Tonight, before I leave.'

'Tonight?' She gaped at him. 'But I only just... Why so quickly?'

'Because I want to prove what I just said to you. I want you to know that I meant every word. I don't know how long it will take me to fulfil my oath to my brothers, but I want to make another to you. I want you and everyone to know that I'm coming back, even if I have to swim the sea with one arm.' He clasped her hands tighter. 'I'll come back and I won't ever tell you how to live your life again. We'll make decisions together.'

'All right, I'll marry you.' She laughed incredulously. 'Tonight.'

'Hilda?' He called out his stepmother's name though he didn't take his eyes off Sissa.

'Well, I'm glad to see you took my advice for once.' Hilda emerged from the hall to join them.

'I did...' he smiled '...and excellent advice it was. Now, what would you say to planning a wedding feast tonight?'

'I'd say don't be ridiculous. It'll be dark before long.'

'But can it be done?'

'It could.' Hilda's jaw dropped as she looked between them. 'You mean...? Stars, Danr, you never do anything by half.' She reached for Sissa's arm, pulling her away. 'Come on, we'll go straight to the bathhouse.'

'What? Why?' Sissa looked at her in surprise.

'Because it's tradition. One of them anyway. We won't have time for most of the others, but we'll do our best. We only have a few hours.'

'No, we have one hour.' Danr's voice was firm. 'If I'm leaving tomorrow, then I want to spend as much time as possible during the rest of today with my wife.' His gaze fastened on hers. 'One hour, then we'll be married.'

An hour, Danr discovered, could be a long time. A *very* long time, especially when a man had just declared his love, was leaving imminently and when every moment was precious. Short of storming the bathhouse, however, there wasn't much he could do about it, especially when Joarr, Knut and half-a-dozen other warriors insisted that he perform his own purifying ritual with a bracing dip in the sea loch. Still, he had to concede it was all worth the sacrifice when he caught his next glimpse of Sissa. She looked breathtaking, dressed in an ankle-length blue gown with a pale yellow over-tunic, held in place by two silver brooches at the shoulders and with a loop of amber beads slung between. Her hair had been combed into submission, too, topped with a silver bridal crown in the shape of intertwining leaves that made her look even more like a forest queen.

The wedding ceremony itself was brief, with a simple exchange of rings, and the celebrations muted at his request. After what had happened in Maerr, weddings themselves had lost their appeal for him and it was hard to celebrate after what they'd just discovered about Kolga and Thorfinn. More than that, he didn't want Sissa to feel any more uncomfortable than she obviously already did around so many people. The tension in her body had been clear all through the ceremony. When he'd slid the wedding band over her finger, it had felt stiff as wood.

'I want to go outside.' Sissa announced finally, leaning sideways across the high bench towards him.

'Whatever you wish.' He stood up, draining the last of the mead from the marriage horn before holding out a hand.

'You're leaving already?' Hilda looked up in surprise. 'Half the hall is still eating.'

'Ah, but I'm not used to being indoors any more. I need air, Stepmother,' Danr answered, ignoring Joarr's pointed grin as he inclined his head towards Knut. 'My thanks for the feast. We're honoured by your hospitality.'

'It's our honour.' Knut raised his own drinking horn. 'You're both welcome here for as long as you wish.'

'My thanks.' Danr put a hand on the small of Sissa's back, guiding her beyond the doors of the hall, collecting a pair of fur cloaks on the way, then heading on through the village, out of the gates and on to the stony shore beyond. Darkness had already fallen, but the moon was high and the stars were shimmering brightly, lighting a path for them.

'Is that better?' He stopped halfway across the beach

to face her. Some intuition told him to keep his distance and give her time to recover, though the urge to touch her was hard to resist.

'Much.' She looked out towards the sea and exhaled, as if she'd been holding her breath all evening.

'Thank you, Sissa. I know that wasn't easy for you.'

'No. There were so many people...' She took another deep breath and then leaned towards him, tucking her head beneath his chin. 'But it wasn't as bad as I'd feared.'

'I'm glad.' He put a tentative hand on her waist. 'That's always a good thing for a wedding.'

'You know what I mean.'

'I do.' He bent his head and pressed a kiss into her hair.

'Will your family mind that you married without their consent? Your brothers might object.'

'They won't.'

'I don't have any dowry. No riches at all.'

'Neither do I. In terms of wealth, we both made a bad bargain, but in the ways that really matter...' he reached up and rubbed his thumbs gently across her cheeks, sliding his fingertips into her hair so that her face was cradled between his hands '... I consider myself a very rich man.'

'A very rich *mate*,' she corrected him, closing her eyes as he kissed her, first on the forehead, then on the tip of her nose, then softly and tenderly on her lips.

'Sissa...' He broke away after a few moments, pressing his forehead against hers. 'You know that I still can't lie with you until...'

'Until you've fulfilled your oath, I know.'

'Yes, but there are things I could…do for you.' He hesitated, wondering if he ought to just suggest they go back inside and sleep instead. The last thing he wanted after such a long day was to shock her.

'What kind of things?'

'Well, there's one thing I've wanted to do for a long time now, or what feels like a long time anyway, but it's easier to show you. Come with me?' He waited until she nodded before slipping a hand into hers and leading her towards the forest.

'Where are we going?'

'Not far.' He stopped when they reached the trees, pulling her into his arms and letting his mouth find hers again. 'It's nothing to be afraid of.'

'I'm not afraid,' she answered breathlessly between kisses. 'I trust you.'

'Good.' He tipped her backwards, lowering them gently on to a bed of pine needles. 'And you can tell me to stop whenever you wish.'

'Danr?' Her expression was confused as he drew her gown up around her thighs, sliding a hand between her legs. 'You said you couldn't…?'

'I know. I'm not,' he whispered against her throat, trailing a line of kisses down her body as she sighed and stretched out beneath him. He growled with anticipation, sliding down between her thighs while his fingers played in the curls between her legs. At last his mouth found her most intimate place and touched gently, moving in small circles over her skin. She stiffened at once, though she didn't object, relaxing after a few moments before starting to move along with him, her whole body arching and bucking and then finally stiffening again as she cried out in the darkness.

Afterwards he gathered her into his arms, holding her tight as she continued to quiver and tremble against him.

'Sissa?' He murmured her name after a few moments, smiling as she pressed her face into his neck drowsily.

'Mmm?'

'I have a favour to ask.' He hesitated. After the trust she'd just shown in allowing him to touch her, he felt faintly guilty about what he was about to say. But he still had to say it. 'It's important to me.'

'Is it something I won't like?'

'Perhaps. Probably. But it won't be for long.'

She sighed languorously. 'If I agree, will you do what you just did again?'

'If you want.' He chuckled. 'All night if you like.'

She tilted her head back. 'Why doesn't that break your oath? Isn't it mating?'

'Not exactly.' He rolled on top of her again. 'Not that I didn't enjoy it, but you've no idea how much I'm torturing myself right now.'

'All right.' She smiled lazily and looped her arms around his neck. 'If you do it again, then I'll do your favour. What is it?'

'Stay here. Until I get back from Eireann, stay in the village. Ow!' He fell backwards as she wrenched her hands away from his neck and shoved him hard in the chest. 'Wait, hear me out.'

'No! How could you ask after everything you said before?'

'I know.' He made a grab for her waist, pulling her back down into his lap as she tried to get up. 'That's why I'm only asking. It's a request, not a demand.'

'I'm not comfortable here, you know that! I don't want to wear fine clothes and eat in a hall and…*talk*!' She shoved her fist into his shoulder this time. 'I want to go home.'

'It won't be for long.'

'You don't *know* how long you'll be gone!'

'I'll come back here before I go anywhere with Brandt, I promise. Then we'll talk again. Please Sissa, I can't go to Eireann knowing you're out in the wilderness all by yourself.'

'I've been by myself for three years!'

'I know that, too.' He held tight as she wriggled against him. 'But I'll be gone for a week, maybe two, at the most, if the weather stays fair.'

'And if the snow comes?'

'Then all the more reason for you to stay here.'

'I'm ready for winter.'

'It's still dangerous on your own.'

'What about Tove and Halvar? They can't stay in the village.'

'No, but Halvar's just looking for an excuse to go and take his mate with him.' He brushed his lips against the back of her neck. 'Maybe it's time to let them go, Sissa. I won't ask any more favours. Just stay here until I get back, for my peace of mind. Please.'

Chapter Twenty-Two

'Thorfinn and Kolga?' Sandulf was the first to speak after a long and ominous silence.

Danr nodded grimly, looking around at each of his brothers in turn. They were standing in a circle in Alarr's private chamber, the first time they'd all been in the same room together in two years.

'You're certain about this?' Brandt folded his arms, a deep frown puckering his brow.

'Yes. Hilda doesn't want to believe it, but the more I think about it, the more likely it seems. Whoever arranged the attack knew what they were doing. They knew all about us, too. And who stood to gain the most in the long run? Kolga claimed Maerr for Eithr, but who acts as his guardian?'

'Her husband.' Rurik pushed a hand through his hair. 'Kolga was always a miserable, bitter woman, but to kill Ingrid and Gilla so brutally... Maybe Thorfinn compelled her somehow? Or maybe he acted alone?

If she had the pendants, then he could easily have taken them.'

'So what now?' Alarr's gaze focused on Brandt. 'You know we'll do whatever you ask of us, Brother.'

'Now I go and confront Thorfinn.' Brandt's voice was like thunder, a deep rumble heralding a gathering storm. 'Rurik's right. It seems more likely to be him than Kolga herself. I need to go and find out.'

'You mean *we* will?'

'No. This part I do alone.'

'Brandt…'

'Alone.' The tone of his voice refused to brook any argument. 'If Thorfinn's responsible for Ingrid's death, then this is between me and him.'

'Very well then.' Alarr gave him a long look. 'You go alone, but only on condition that you summon us if you need to. We'll all come, wherever we are.'

'This is madness.' Danr stepped forward angrily. 'It's too dangerous for Brandt to go alone. This isn't *just* his fight. It belongs to all of us.'

'Not any more.' Brandt's expression was resolute. 'If I fail, then the rest of you can come and finish what I start, but I go first. You've done your part, Danr, but it's time for you to let it go.'

'Not until I make things right.'

'You can't. No one can do that.' Brandt laid a hand on his shoulder, the look in his eyes softening slightly. 'But you *have* made them better. It's time to stop punishing yourself.'

Danr clenched his jaw. 'I still failed you. I should have been in the hall that day.'

'But you weren't and the assassins were worried enough about your skill with a sword to make sure you weren't. I'm just glad they did it with a woman and not with a dagger. Then I would have lost a brother, too.'

'And I would have lost my twin.' Rurik grasped his other shoulder.

'And who would have saved my life in Strathclyde?' Sandulf smiled. 'We don't blame you for surviving, Brother.'

'You can really forgive me?' He looked around at them each in turn.

'We can. Whatever mistakes you've made, you've paid for them.' Alarr gave a nod of support. 'Now you need to get on with your life.'

'With other things, too.' Sandulf smirked. 'Since this means you've fulfilled your oath.'

'What oath?' Alarr looked between them both curiously. 'Danr? Sandulf?'

'It's not my business.' Sandulf shrugged his shoulders and then stared pointedly at the ceiling. 'But you won't believe it. I could hardly believe it. *No one* from Maerr would believe it.'

'What?' Brandt, Alarr and Rurik all spoke together.

'No women.' Danr threw a vengeful look at Sandulf and then cleared his throat. 'I swore that I wouldn't lie with a woman until I'd made amends and earned your forgiveness.'

'*You* made an oath of celibacy?' Rurik sounded disbelieving.

'Yes.'

'When?'

'After the massacre.'

'But that was three years ago.'

'You don't need to remind me.'

'And you've kept to your oath for three years?'

'Yes!'

'So you're saying that *you*…' Rurik paused for effect '…*you*, my brother Danr Sigurdsson, haven't lain with a woman in…three years?'

'It's not *that* unlikely.' He was starting to get annoyed. 'And it's not funny, either.'

'Yes, it is.'

'Well, apparently people really can change.' Alarr let out a low whistle.

'I knew you could do it.' Sandulf slapped him on the back with a laugh. 'I had total confidence in you.'

'Then what are you still doing here with us?' Even Brandt was smiling. 'Half the maids in Alarr's hall gawked at you when you came in. Go and find one!'

'Or two.' Sandulf chuckled. 'Only don't tell Ceanna I said that.'

'No,' Danr answered quietly.

'No?' Alarr lifted his eyebrows. 'Don't tell me you've forgotten how to do it, Brother? Because if you want some advice…'

'I don't want just *any* woman.' He planted his feet firmly apart as they all stared at him. 'I only want one woman. My wife.'

'Wife?' Rurik's jaw fell open again.

'Yes. Her name's Sissa and I married her just before I left Skíð. She's staying with Hilda until I return. What?' He frowned as they all exchanged looks.

'Hilda? Our mother and your stepmother Hilda?' Brandt spoke first. 'I thought the two of you hated each other?'

'We do. *Did.*' He shrugged. 'We're trying not to any more.'

'So let me get this clear.' Rurik placed a fraternal arm around his shoulders. 'Not only have you committed yourself to one woman—for life—but you want to return to Skíð to live on the same island as our stepmother?'

'Yes, Sissa and Hilda seem to get along. But we're not going to *live* with her. We're going to live in the forest.'

'The forest?'

'Sissa has a roundhouse. It's small, but she has a cave, too. She's a healer.'

'Ah.' Rurik exchanged another look with the others. 'Is she beautiful?'

'Not in an obvious way.' He smiled at the question. 'The first time I saw her she had clay on her face and her hair looked like a bird's nest.'

'Is her body…?' Rurik gestured at his chest.

'She says she looks like a tree. I've always thought her more like a spear.'

'Is she biddable?'

'No.' He could feel the smile widening across his face. 'She once hit me with the hilt of a dagger so hard I almost passed out.'

'Does she laugh at your jokes?'

'Sometimes. She likes my stories, but a lot of the time she'd rather sit quietly with her wolves.'

'Wolves?'

'She has two. Halvar and Tove. You know, Halvar reminds me of you.'

'Danr…' Rurik sounded serious now. 'Are you sure you're all right?'

'I am.' He laughed outright. 'For the first time in a long time, I really am. I'm in love.'

'Then I'm happy for you.' Rurik smiled, too. 'She sounds interesting. Unique.'

'She is.'

'But you and she haven't…?' Alarr let the question hang in the air.

'Not yet.'

'You'll be leaving in the morning then?'

'On the very first tide, yes.'

'Aren't you tired?' Danr found his eldest brother standing outside the hall, alone in the darkness. It had been a long night of feasting, but most of the revellers had finally gone to bed or collapsed in drunken stupors, Alarr, Rurik and Sandulf among them.

'I've been thinking.' Brandt's voice was heavy.

'About Kolga and Thorfinn?'

'Yes. He has a stronghold in Katanes. I'll go there next.'

'You know I'll still come with you if you need me to. It might be—'

'No.' Brandt interrupted him firmly. 'And no more arguments.' He gave him an appraising look. 'Why aren't you sleeping? You've had a long journey.'

'Because right now I'd rather talk to you.'

There was a sound of feminine laughter from the doorway behind them, obviously designed to be enticing, and Brandt jerked his head in that direction. 'Still not tempted? Your woman would never know.'

'But *I* would.'

Brandt gave a smile of approval. 'She must be special, your healer.'

'She is. She survived on her own in the wilderness for years. I've never met anyone like her before.'

'You really love her, then?'

'With all my heart.'

Brandt nodded thoughtfully. 'Ingrid said you'd fall in love one day.'

Danr stiffened. It was the first time he'd heard Brandt say his dead wife's name aloud since the day of the massacre. 'She did?'

'Yes, and that when you finally fell for a woman you'd fall hard. It seems she was right. She always did have a soft spot for you.' Brandt gave him a glower that turned into a smile. 'She said there was more to you than most people saw.'

'I hope she was right.'

'She was. You were the one who refused to acknowledge it, not us.'

'You know, I cared about Ingrid, too. She was beautiful inside and out. I would have died before I let anything happen to her. If I'd been there…'

'I know.' Brandt tilted his head, looking up at the stars. 'She would have known it, too. But she wouldn't have wanted you to be killed that day either. She would have wanted you to live and be happy. She would have

been glad that you've found someone. Just like I am—
for all my brothers. You've all found partners who
suit you.'

'Maybe one day…'

'No.' Brandt's voice hardened. 'There won't be anyone else for me. All I want now is justice for Ingrid.'

They were silent for a few moments before Brandt
lowered his head again. 'If we're leaving in the morning, then I suppose I should pack.'

'We?'

'Skíð is on the way to Katanes. It's probably time I
spoke to my mother and I wouldn't miss meeting this
wife of yours for the world.' He laughed. 'Sandulf was
right; no one from Maerr would ever believe it. Danr
Sigurdsson, in love.'

'There you are.' Hilda came bustling across the hall,
a green tunic draped over one arm. 'This will suit you
perfectly.'

'What is it for?' Sissa looked up from her sewing,
taking the garment and holding it out at arm's length in
confusion. It was undeniably beautiful, with a neckline
and cuffs trimmed with intricately woven green and
yellow braid which had obviously taken many hours
to make, but it was far *too* fine for living in a forest.
Impractical, too. She'd wrench the sleeves off within
a day.

'For you to wear, of course. And we'd better start
braiding your hair properly now that you're a married
woman.' Hilda smiled benevolently. 'You want Danr
to be pleased when he sees you.'

'He knows what I look like.' Sissa lifted an eyebrow, surprised by the other woman's enthusiasm. 'You really don't hate him any more, do you?'

'No.' Hilda sat down on a stool by her side. 'I'm tired of all that. I was tired of it a long time ago, but I didn't know how to let go of it. Now I want to think of the future and the village we're going to build.'

'Village?' She dropped the gown into her lap abruptly.

'Didn't Danr tell you?' Hilda gave a secretive smile. 'I suppose it was all such a rush before he left. Joarr wants us to build a new hall somewhere close by on the island.'

'No, he didn't mention anything.' She searched her memory, but he hadn't said a word about building a hall, at least not since that night when they'd camped on the other side of the island and that had only been a passing thought, surely? 'You mean Danr discussed it with you?'

'Only briefly, but he thought it was a good idea.'

'I didn't think you and he would *want* to live in the same village.'

Hilda made a dismissive sound. 'I admit the idea seemed unlikely to me, too, at first, but as long as he proves a good husband to you, Danr will be a part of my family from now on. Which makes you my daughter. Truth be told, I always wanted one of those. And I hope you and Danr will have many more for me to enjoy.'

'Many more what?'

'Daughters, of course!' Hilda laughed. 'And sons, too. It'll be good to have children around again.'

'Oh.' Sissa balled her fists into the tunic on her lap. She hadn't planned *that* far ahead. She hadn't planned at all beyond Danr's return. She'd only just accepted the idea of sharing her life with him. She *definitely* hadn't considered children!

'But there's plenty of time for all that…' Hilda continued, 'though I don't suppose Danr will want to waste any time getting started.'

'You mean with mating?'

'I…' Hilda's expression froze with an expression of shock. 'Ye-es, I suppose so… Ah.' She stood up hastily. 'I see Alva wants me. We'll talk more later.'

Sissa watched her go, squeezing her brows together and chewing the insides of her cheek anxiously. The tunic in her lap felt heavy. No doubt Hilda wanted her to try it on, but she didn't want to. All she wanted was to get out into the open air, away from the bustle and noise of the hall where the very walls felt as though they were closing in and stifling her senses. *A village?* Danr had said they'd make decisions together. He definitely hadn't said anything about a village, but according to Hilda, they'd already agreed and her future was as good as decided. They were going to build a new village, a new home where she and Danr could live and have babies… *Babies!*

She rubbed her palms together as they started to sweat. Her head was swimming, although it didn't feel quite like *her* head either. She felt as if she were outside her own body and looking at someone with neatly combed hair, a clean woollen gown and a freshly scrubbed face. At this rate, Danr might not even recognise her when he came back. *If* he came back.

She stood up, trying to shake off the sense of rising panic. *What if* he never came back? She'd tried not to think about the possibility after his longboat had left, but he'd already been gone for twelve days—surely enough time for him to reach Eireann and come back again? *What if* something had happened to him? *What if* he'd changed his mind about being married to her? *What if* Hilda had been right about him all along?

She started up out of her seat, the tunic sliding from her fingers to the floor. How long was she supposed to wait? Surely two weeks was as long as Danr could have expected? It wasn't as if she was *really* in any danger on her own. She'd survived for three years without any help. Besides, if she left now he wouldn't know anything about it until he came back and if he was angry with her then, well, what would it matter at that point? According to Hilda, *he* was planning to break his word about where they would live, so why shouldn't *she* break hers? She'd done the favour he'd asked for as long as she could bear it, but she didn't have to stay for ever. If that was the kind of wife he wanted, then he ought to have chosen one of his other women.

The thought of *them* steeled her resolve. She'd made a mistake in agreeing to his favour. In agreeing to marry him at all, perhaps. She wasn't suited to life in a hall, around people. She was suited to being on her own and taking care of herself.

The forest was her home, the place where she belonged. That was where she would go.

Chapter Twenty-Three

Skíð

Danr leaped off the prow of the longboat on to the beach. The return journey had taken longer than he'd expected, thanks to a storm that had kept them trapped on shore at first and then blown them too far south, but he was finally back, his feet rooted in the one place in the world that now felt like home. It was raining—*of course* it was raining—but he felt ten times lighter and happier than he had when he'd left. He was back and he was staying. With his wife.

It was an exhilarated feeling that lasted all of thirty seconds until he lifted his head and saw Hilda running across the beach towards him, her expression a combination of relief and dread.

'What's happened?' He grasped hold of her upper arms as she reached him. 'Where's Sissa?'

'I don't know. She's run away... *Brandt?*'

'Mother.' His brother's customary scowl became

even more pronounced at the sight of Joarr striding up behind her.

'What do you mean, she's run away?' Danr tightened his grip on her shoulders. Whatever she had to discuss with Brandt could wait. 'What happened?'

'I don't know. One moment I was giving her a gown and talking about the future, the next she was gone. The guards said she just walked out and left.'

'What? When?'

'Two days ago.'

'Two days?' He frowned. Why would she have left? Especially after she'd promised him? Had she deceived him—*tricked him*—again? No. He discarded the idea as quickly as he thought it. If she'd never intended to stay, then she would have left straight away, as soon as his boat was out of sight. There had to be another reason and at least two days wasn't long. She couldn't have gone far.

'She's probably just gone back to her roundhouse,' he said with relief.

'We've been into the forest.' It was Joarr who spoke this time. 'We found her roundhouse, but there was no sign of her. No sign of anyone having been there for a while either.'

'Halvar? Tove?' He made an impatient gesture as everyone stared at him blankly. 'Her wolves! Did you see them?'

'Not a glimpse.'

Danr looked towards the forest, struck with a growing sense of unease. He felt as if there were icy fingers trailing up and down his spine, warning him something was wrong. Where was she this time? Wherever it was, he only hoped that Halvar and Tove were with her, protecting her, unless they'd simply wandered away after she'd agreed to stay in the village, as he'd thought they might. His stomach churned at the thought.

'I don't know what happened.' Hilda reached for his sleeve. 'She was quiet while she was here, but there didn't seem to be anything wrong. I'm sorry.'

'You said you were talking about the future right before she left. What kind of future?'

'Just about the hall we're going to build.'

'Wait, you mean you told her about your plans for a new village? Did you say I was involved?'

'Just that you thought it was a good idea.' She bit her lip. 'Although, I suppose I might have implied more. I said it would be a good place to raise children.'

'Children?'

'Yes.' Hilda looked stricken. 'Do you think I frightened her away?'

Yes!

He bit his tongue on the word, squeezing her shoulders reassuringly instead. The gesture would have been unthinkable two weeks ago, but now he knew the concern in her eyes was genuine. And *he* wasn't blameless. He should have asked Hilda not to mention the new village, especially after he'd promised Sissa they would make decisions together. Now she probably thought he'd been planning behind her back, planning to tell her what to do again. Panic clawed at his throat, so he had to take a deep breath before he spoke again.

'I need to go and look for her. She might have gone along the coast.'

'We've been that way, too.' Joarr sounded sombre. 'We've searched all along the shore.'

'What about to the east, through the mountain pass?'

'To the other side of the island? Why would she go that way?'

'Because it's the only other place I can think of.' His heart leapt at the idea. 'I need a horse. It'll be quicker if I ride.'

'There's more bad weather coming.' Joarr gestured towards the horizon.

'The weather is the reason I need to go.' He remembered the perilous ridge over the mountain and shuddered. 'She might be trapped somewhere or hurt.'

'She knows how to take care of herself.'

'I know, but I can't just stay here and wait.'

'Then I'd better go with you.' Brandt looked grimly at his mother. 'We'll talk later. Right now we need horses and supplies.'

'I'll see to it.' Joarr nodded.

'Hurry!' Danr was already running up the beach. 'We need to leave now!'

Sissa lifted her head, examining the pile of rotten timber lying over her body in case she'd missed some obvious way out, then dropped it again despairingly. It was no use. Her arms and legs were trapped and there was no way for her to wriggle out. The shelf she'd been reaching for had given way beneath her fingertips, pulling down what was left of the wall and roof along with it. She supposed she ought to be grateful that the beams had missed her head and that she was pinned to the ground, rather than crushed. None of her limbs felt as though they were injured, but heave as she might, there was no way for her to dislodge the wood covering her all the way from her neck down to her toes.

She sighed. She hadn't even intended to come here, only once she'd got back to the clearing, she'd calmed down enough to realise that she'd overreacted. There was no proof that Danr had lied. Any discussion he might have had about a new village with Hilda had likely been just that, a discussion. It wasn't as if he would have been able to *force* her to live there anyway. It was probably just an idea and maybe—the thought had gradually occurred to her as she'd walked—maybe it wasn't such a bad one. Maybe it really *was* time for her to start living with people again. In which case there was something she'd wanted to do first.

That was the reason she'd come here, on her own and without telling anyone, which with hindsight had *definitely* been a mistake. It was ironic. She'd come back to the site of her first home to say goodbye to the past and found herself trapped beneath it instead. Unfortunately, it wasn't the slightest bit funny.

'I know. I shouldn't have come.' She turned her head to look at Tove, lying beside her, and then Halvar, a few feet away. 'But I'm glad you're both here.'

In truth, she was more than glad. Hunger and a painfully dry throat were bad enough, but the last night of utter blackness would have been well-nigh unbearable without their company.

'I should have told Hilda where I was going,' she went on regretfully, 'but I thought she'd try to stop me. It was foolish, but I meant to go back. You believe me, don't you?'

She sighed and looked up at the sky where yet more grey clouds were massing, threatening rain and worse. The temperature was already plummeting, making her shiver despite her fur cloak. Every time she breathed in she felt as though her lungs were filling with ice. It wouldn't be long before she was either drenched or buried in snow. Just like the way she'd found Danr, she realised, her heart clenching at the thought. Where was he now? Still in Eireann probably, or maybe on his journey back, too far away to rescue her. When he returned to Skíð, they'd tell him that she'd gone, without a clue as to why or where. He'd search for her, but what if he thought she'd lied and tricked him again? And who could blame him? All he'd know was that she'd broken her promise and left.

'You need to slow down!' Brandt bellowed behind him.

'I can't!' Danr didn't look around, icy blasts of air whipping across his face as he leaned over his mount's neck, thundering through yet another valley.

'Yes, you can, or in this terrain your horse will stumble and then we'll have to make our way on foot.' Brandt charged up beside him and grabbed hold of his horse's bridle. 'I know how you feel, Brother, but you need to calm down. Getting yourself injured won't help her.'

Danr gritted his teeth, resisting the urge to spur his horse on anyway. 'It's not that easy. I just…'

'*I know.*'

He twisted his head at the sound of pain in his brother's voice. For the first time, he realised how hard this must be for Brandt, racing to find a woman, just as he'd raced to save Ingrid…

'I'm sorry. I shouldn't have let you come.'

'You couldn't have stopped me. Where are we going anyway?'

'To her old village. It was almost completely destroyed by outlaws five years ago, but she still goes there sometimes. It's the only place I can think of.'

'How much further?'

'Too far. We're going to get wet.'

'I can live with wet.' Brandt gestured behind them, to where lightning was already streaking the horizon. '*That's* what I'm worried about. We'll need to find shelter soon.'

'No.' Danr clenched his jaw grimly. 'I'm not stopping. I'll ride through a storm if I have to.'

'I believe you, Brother.' Brandt held on to his gaze for a long moment and then nodded. 'Let's go, then.'

Chapter Twenty-Four

The rain started some time around what Sissa guessed was mid-afternoon, a light drizzle at first that turned swiftly into a torrential downpour, soaking through her fur cloak and into her skin. She shivered violently. What was it that Danr had said about the rain never stopping on Skíð? It had actually rained less than usual while he'd been there, as if his presence had brought sunshine back into her life for a while, which, fanciful though it sounded, was true. His arrival *had* brightened her days. Now he was gone, it was only fitting that the dark clouds were back and apparently determined to make up for lost time.

A raindrop hit her in one eye and she winced, turning her head so that one side of her face was protected at least. Beside her, Tove whimpered, as if she felt helpless, too, but at least she was all right. Sissa smiled and made a small murmur of reassurance. That was one consolation. No matter what happened to her, at least Tove would survive. Halvar would take care of her.

She glanced at the male wolf, surprised to see him prick up his ears and then raise himself on his front paws suddenly.

'What is it?' She tried not to feel hopeful. It was probably just an otter or deer passing by, she told herself, though if it was then apparently it could speak. If she wasn't imagining things, she could hear shouting in the distance.

'Sissa?'

Her heart leapt at the sound of Danr's voice. She would have recognised it anywhere.

'In here!' she shouted back as loudly as she could through parched lips though it wasn't loud enough. Fortunately, Halvar howled for her, guiding Danr towards them while she held her breath, waiting, willing him to be real and not a figment of her imagination. It seemed like an eternity passed until she heard footsteps and he appeared around the edge of the half-collapsed longhouse.

'Sissa.' He vaulted over the fallen planks to reach her. 'What happened? Are you hurt?'

'Questions later.' Another man, a giant with dark hair and familiar-looking blue eyes, accompanied him. 'Let's get her out first.'

'No. Wait.' Her heart lifted as she looked up into Danr's face. 'I love you. I should have said it before you left, but I do.'

'You love me?' His gaze looked arrested.

'Even more than I did when you left.'

'Lift!' The other man gestured to the uppermost beam. 'After three.'

'I love you even more, too.' Danr sounded apologetic. 'But this might hurt.'

'I don't care. Just get me out.'

'One, two…'

They made quick work of the beam, tossing it away and then wrenching the other planks aside as if they were simply playing some bigger version of knuckle sticks.

'Can you feel your legs?' Danr reached down, skimming his hands gently over her limbs.

'Yes.' She heaved herself up on her elbows. 'I was only pinned down. I don't think anything was broken or crushed.'

'We need to get you out of here.'

'One of the other buildings looks reasonably sturdy.' The other man frowned. 'It's not the best idea considering what happened here, but we need shelter. I'll go and have a closer look.' He started away and then stopped. 'About the wolves…?'

'They won't hurt you.' Danr slid his arms behind her knees and shoulders. 'They know you're with us.'

'If you say so.'

'Hold on to me,' Danr murmured, gathering her against him and carrying her across the ruins of the old village. The rain was coming down in sheets now, soaking them both to the bone—just when she'd thought it was impossible to get any wetter! Still, at this moment she found it hard to care. Just seeing him again felt too good to be true.

'What are you doing here?' she asked in wonderment.

'What am *I* doing here?' He gave her an exasperated look. 'What are *you* doing here? You promised to stay with Hilda.'

'I know, but you were gone for so long.'

'Two weeks.'

'It felt longer.' She bit her lip guiltily. 'But I was going to go back. It wasn't another trick, I promise.'

'I know.' He lowered her down to the ground as soon as they were inside the last reasonably solid longhouse, where the other man was already inspecting the rafters. 'That doesn't matter now, but what were you were thinking, coming here alone, without telling anyone? You don't have to do everything alone any more, Sissa.'

'I know. I'm sorry.'

'Sorry?' Danr removed his cloak and draped it around her shoulders, soggy as it was. 'Sorry isn't good enough. Here, drink this.' He handed her a flask of ale. 'And don't think you—'

'Are you one of his brothers?' she interrupted, glancing towards the other man, unwilling to be scolded in front of an audience.

'I'm Brandt.'

'The one who threatened to cut out his tongue?'

'The same.' His lips almost, but not quite, twitched. 'Not that threatening him ever worked.'

'I know. I'm Sissa.'

'My new sister, I guessed.' He looked her over with interest. 'Let him bluster for a bit. He was truly worried. He almost lamed himself and two horses trying to get here.'

'Really?'

'What do you think?' Danr sounded angry now.

'Hilda said you just walked out of the village one day and then Joarr said there was no sign of you in the forest. I was afraid you might have fallen off a mountainside or something.' His expression became anguished. 'If we hadn't arrived back when we did...'

'I'll go and find some firewood.' Brandt made for the doorway again.

'I really am sorry.' Sissa reached for Danr's hand. 'I shouldn't have left.'

'No, you shouldn't. Was it *so* hard being around people?'

She made a face. 'It wasn't easy, but then Hilda mentioned us building a hall and having children...' She swallowed. 'I panicked. I thought that maybe you'd lied about not telling me what to do. That's why I went back to the forest. Only once I got there, I decided to trust you instead. I was going to go back, but I wanted to come here first.'

The angry look in his eye softened. 'Why?'

'To fetch something.' She reached into her cloak and pulled out a wooden *tafl* figure. 'My father carved this king when I was a girl. All the things I took from here belonged to other people. I never took anything from my own home. It was too painful to be reminded of my family.'

'And now?'

'Now I want to move on—and you kept saying we needed a game. I thought we could add this to the pieces you've already carved.' There was a roll of thunder in the distance and she made a face. 'Although I admit this probably wasn't the best time to come.'

'At least I found you. I've never been so scared in my whole life as I've been in the past few hours. Even that day in Maerr.' He cupped her face in his hands, pressing his lips to her forehead and pulling her close. 'Do you really love me?'

'I do.' She nuzzled her face against his neck. 'Enough to live in a hall if that's what you want?'

'Who said I want that?'

'No one, but—'

'I told you, we'll make decisions together, and we'll live wherever *you* want. In a tree or a cave or...'

'Here.'

'Here?' He looked around at the dilapidated building.

'Well, not here, exactly, but close by. You said it was a good position. We could build our own longhouse.'

'I'll build you ten longhouses if that's what you really want.' He grinned. 'And we'll just go back to the forest whenever Hilda and I want to kill each other.'

'So every other day?' She laughed. 'That sounds perfect.'

'Sissa.' The look in his eyes heated as he placed one hand beneath her chin, tilting it upwards so he could lower his lips to hers...

'Ahem.' Brandt cleared his throat loudly as he came back in, his arms laden with branches that he proceeded to drop in the old hearth. 'These are the driest I could find, which isn't saying much. We'll just have to hope they light.' A look of amusement crossed his features. 'If it's not hot enough in here already?'

Fortunately, after several minutes of futile strikes,

a small flame flickered into life, accompanied by a growl of satisfaction from Brandt.

'Come, you need to walk around, get some blood flowing back through your legs.' Danr grasped hold of her elbows, levering her back to her feet.

'I know.' She stood up carefully and stretched up on her toes a few times. 'But I feel all right.'

'Are you certain?' He still looked concerned. 'Maybe I should take a look?'

'Truly, I'm all right.' Sissa smiled reassuringly, surprised by a snorting sound from the other side of the fire.

'Well, you must still be hungry.' Danr threw a swift glare at his brother and then reached into his pack for some bread. 'Here. Eat this.'

Ten minutes later, they were all gathered around the fire, listening to the rain lashing overhead.

'I always thought Maerr was bad for rain.' Brandt peered outside. 'But this place might be even worse.'

'Are you going back there?' Sissa looked towards him with interest. 'Now that Danr's told you what we discovered about your aunt.'

'I'll get to Maerr eventually. First I'm going to Katanes, to visit her new husband. He has a fortress there.'

'So you think he's involved?'

Brandt nodded, lifting a skin of ale to his lips. 'We've exhausted every other possibility. This is the only one that makes sense. I need to travel there before winter sets in.'

'Just you? You mean you're going alone?' She looked at Danr hopefully and he wrapped an arm around her.

'I'm not going anywhere. My brothers have forgiven me.'

'So your oath…'

'Is fulfilled.' His eyes darkened as they gazed into hers. 'I'm back for good.'

'Then that means we can mate now?'

This time the noise sounded like spluttering from the other side of the fire.

'You must be getting old, Brother.' Danr grinned, though he never moved his eyes from her face. 'It seems you can't handle your ale any more.'

'I'm going to check on the horses.' Brandt got to his feet, muttering something that sounded suspiciously like he was comparing his brother to sheep dung. 'I'll be back in an hour. No more, understand?'

'Perfectly. Take the ale.'

'What did you think I was going to do?'

'It's still raining,' Sissa protested as he disappeared through the gap in the wall. 'What about the storm?'

'Don't worry about him.' Danr sounded unconcerned. 'He'll find shelter somewhere.'

'But—' She went silent as his lips touched upon hers again, kissing her with a tenderness that left her breathless.

'What about nothing,' he murmured against her mouth after a few mind-spinning moments. 'A man can only endure for so long and I can't keep my hands off you any longer.'

'Neither can I.' She gave a smile of assent and slid

her hands up over his forearms, across his broad shoulders and then around his neck, forgetting all about Brandt as they lay back on Danr's cloak. He made a low rumbling sound in his throat and a familiar quivering sensation took over her body, first in her stomach, then out through the rest of her limbs, heating her blood and sending tremors of excitement like hot sparks shooting along every nerve.

'I still need to inspect your legs.' He slid a hand beneath the hem of her tunic, caressing the skin beneath. 'Mmm, just as I thought. They definitely need some attention.'

She tipped her head back, closing her eyes in pleasure as he bent his head and started to kiss his way up her legs, beginning with her ankles and gradually moving up between her thighs. She felt her pulse quicken, arching her back as his tongue played lightly over her skin, kissing and licking and nuzzling.

'Danr…' She moaned in frustration.

'You need to get out of these damp clothes,' he told her, lifting himself up just when she thought she couldn't bear the tension any longer. 'Here, let me help.' He drew her tunic up over her head. 'There. *Much* better.'

'But it's cold.'

'Not for long.' He grinned, tearing his own clothes away faster than she would have imagined possible. 'Trust me.'

'I do.' She sighed with satisfaction, relishing the warmth of his body as he lay down over her again, wrapping her legs around his waist to draw him even closer.

'Sissa...' He slid one hand behind her back while the other moved between them, stroking gently into the curls between her legs. 'I want you to be ready.'

'I'm ready.' She pressed her hands against his chest, tracing the shape of every corded muscle. 'I've had to wait, too.'

He gave a low growl, skimming his lips against the side of her throat as he lowered himself against her, pushing gently but insistently at the entrance to her body. Instinctively, she tilted her hips, adjusting the angle and then... She gasped as he entered her, holding completely still as her inner muscles protested. There was a sensation of pain, so much so that she almost changed her mind, and then pleasure gradually returned again, more intense than before. She was aware of him holding still, too, waiting for her to give permission to continue, and she lifted her head, letting her tongue twine with his as she rocked her hips back and forth. They started to both move together, almost leisurely at first, then in a longer, deeper rhythm, a series of smooth glides that made her feel relaxed and tense at the same time. As the pace increased, the tension built even further until all her muscles seemed to clench simultaneously, her stomach contracting to a single coiled point that was both pain and pleasure at the same time. Then heat overwhelmed her, a bursting, blissful feeling accompanied by a trembling sensation that swept away all rational thought and pulsed in hot waves through her body, tearing a cry of release from her throat.

'*Danr,*' she called out and he gave an echoing cry, not quite distinguishable as a name, more like a guttural moan as he stiffened and then shuddered against her.

She closed her eyes, gasping for air and letting her racing heartbeat return to normal as he lay on top of her. He'd been right about one thing. She *definitely* wasn't cold any longer. On the contrary, her body was covered with a thin sheen of perspiration.

'*That* was worth waiting for.' Danr's voice was muffled against her shoulder. 'Did it hurt you?'

He started to move away, but she tightened her arms and legs around him, holding him in place as she stroked her fingers across his back.

'Sissa?'

She opened one eye to find his face just above hers, his expression so anxious that she almost laughed.

'Why are you still talking, Norseman?' She smiled lazily instead.

'Because there are some things a man needs to know, especially from the woman he's just made love to. For the first time.'

'There was some pain at first.' She sighed contentedly. 'But it passed.'

'And the rest?'

'What do *you* think? The rest was everything I could have imagined.' She gave him an arch look. 'And I imagined a lot after our wedding night. But it was even better than that.'

'It was?' He grinned and rolled on to his back, pulling her with him. 'Good. Because I had a hard time restraining myself just now.'

'That was you restraining yourself?'

'You have no idea. Next time you won't be so fortunate.'

'When will that be?'

'Ideally, I'd ask you to give me a few minutes, but you might be sore for a little while.'

'And your brother will be coming back soon...'

'That, too. In that case, I'll try to contain myself, but soon. *Very* soon. I have three years of catching up to do and we're just getting started.'

Chapter Twenty-Five

'Farewell, Brother. Good luck.' Danr enveloped Brandt in a bear hug as they stood on the wooden jetty of the sea loch. It had been two days since they'd returned with Sissa from the other side of the island, bedraggled but unharmed, to the immense relief of everyone in the village, but Hilda especially. Now Knut's longship was manned and waiting to carry Brandt north to Katanes and the mainland. 'Try not to lose your temper.'

'I can't promise anything.' Brandt's expression hardened. Danr had the distinct impression that his mind was already elsewhere, travelling ahead of him to Alba, seeking out ways to gain justice for Ingrid. 'But I'll try.'

'Are you absolutely certain about this? I still don't like you going alone. If you need me...'

'I know, I know, send for you and you'll come. You've told me a hundred times already, but I'm glad to hear it. I might have spent most of our lives telling you to be quiet, but I missed your voice when it was gone. It's good have the old Danr back again.'

'Not quite the old Danr.'

'A better version, then.' The hardness in Brandt's face softened slightly, an almost-smile hovering about his lips. 'And if ever a...*mate* could keep a man on the straight and narrow, I think you've found her. She suits you well, Brother.'

'I know.' Danr grinned. 'I think I suit her, too. Trust me, I won't be wandering away anywhere.'

'I'm glad to hear it.' Brandt inclined his head as Sissa walked along the jetty towards them. 'I'd tell him to take care of you, but I don't suppose I need to, just as long as you keep out of ruins from now on.'

'We'll take care of each other.' She smiled between the two of them.

'That's as it should be. You both need to look to the future now. Leave the past to me.'

'Brandt...' Danr felt a lump swell in his throat.

'No more talk.' Brandt's own voice sounded suspiciously tight. 'I've forgiven you and I've told you to be happy. That's a demand, not a request. Remember that, no matter what happens to me.'

'Thank you, Brother.'

'And do one more thing for me?'

'Anything.'

Brandt glanced towards the end of the jetty, where Hilda was standing beside Joarr. 'Look after my mother. From a safe distance, obviously.'

'Are the two of you reconciled?'

'In a manner of speaking. We talked and I wished her and Joarr well. At least we know he'll treat her better than Father ever did.'

'That won't be hard.'

'No, but this island might not be big enough for the pair of you either. Try not to tear each other's throats out.'

'I'll make sure of it.' Sissa poked Danr in the ribs.

'I'll do my best.' He laughed. 'Safe travels, Brother.'

They embraced one last time before Brandt lifted a hand to Hilda and clambered over the side of the longship.

'Well, then…' Sissa curled an arm around Danr's waist, tipping her head against his shoulder as a dozen oars dipped into the water and the longboat pulled slowly away. 'Shall we do what he said?'

'You mean get on with our lives and be happy? That sounds like a good idea to me.' He raised her other hand to his lips, pressing a kiss against the knuckles. 'It's you and me now. Whatever we do, wherever we go, from now on we do it together.'

'Together.' She snuggled closer and then looked up at him quizzically. 'Why didn't you tell him about our plans for the new village?'

'*Tell him* I'm planning to live in the same place as Hilda?' Danr snorted. 'I'd never live it down. He'd never believe it could work either. *I'm* not even sure it can work.' He shook his head. 'I must be mad, but then I always thought love was a kind of madness.'

'And now?'

'Now I *know* it is, but I also know it's worth it.'

'We won't be building anything until the spring anyway.' She squeezed his waist. 'That means we have the whole winter ahead with just the two of us. We could be stranded in the forest for months.'

'If you're waiting for me to object, then you'll be waiting a long time. It sounds perfect.' He slid a hand over her lower back. 'I'm sure we can think of a few ways to pass the time and stay warm.'

'I'm relying on it. If I remember correctly, you told me once that your hands were famous in Maerr. Not to mention your tongue.'

'And if I remember correctly, you almost stabbed me because of it.'

'Things have changed. Now I expect you to live up to your reputation.' She gave him an arch look. 'When *can* we go back to the forest?'

'Tomorrow, if you like. Then it'll be just you, me and one extremely cosy roundhouse.' He led her back along the jetty. 'And a couple of wolves.'

'You know, when I went back to the clearing after two weeks, Tove and Halvar were both still there. I don't think they're going to leave us, after all.'

'Good.' Danr smiled at the thought. 'That makes us a family.'

'I'd hoped Brandt would stay for longer.' Hilda gave them a mournful look as they approached.

'He wants to reach Katanes before winter sets in.' Danr glanced back over his shoulder to where the long-boat was just sailing around the edge of the sea loch. 'You know it was now or wait until spring.'

'Did he sleep at all last night? The two of you were up late talking.'

'*Too* late.' Danr yawned. 'I don't think he sleeps much any more.'

'No. I wish there was something I could have said or done to comfort him, but he seems so weighed down with burdens.'

'Who can blame him after what happened?' Joarr sounded sombre. 'He lost the woman he loved as well as his birthright. I hope he finds a way to reclaim his kingdom, but I don't see how.'

'I hope so, too.' Sissa nodded. 'He needs to find peace again.'

'If anyone can do it, it's Brandt. You know he was always as stubborn as an ox.' Danr glanced slyly at Hilda, trying to lighten the mood. 'I can't imagine where he gets it from.'

'Mmm...' She gave him a suspicious look. 'Your father *was* always pig-headed. And you're not immune to the fault, Danr Sigurdsson.'

'True.' He waited a couple of seconds before adopting a deliberately casual tone. 'By the way, Brandt asked me to look after you.'

'What?' Her eyes widened. 'But I have Joarr to do that!'

'None the less...' Danr shrugged '... I promised. Which means from now on, I'll be like your shadow. Always following. Always watching. Any time you as much as trip or stumble, I'll be there to catch you...'

'You will not. As if I need *you*!'

'A promise is a promise, Stepmother.' Danr gave her a wicked grin, eliciting a weary groan from Joarr.

'Is this what we have to look forward to, the two

of you bickering constantly? Because if it is then we should build *two* villages. As far away from each other as possible.'

'We're not bickering.' To Danr's amazement, Hilda gave him what looked like a conspiratorial smile. 'We're enjoying ourselves.'

'Stars help me.'

'Don't worry.' Danr slipped his hand into Sissa's. 'We're going back to the forest for the winter anyway. You won't have to put up with me for a while, but if you do need me...' He paused, hardly able to believe he was actually saying the words. 'You know where to find me.'

'Thank you.' Hilda looked as surprised as he felt. 'Well, then, when do you intend to leave?'

'Tomorrow.'

'Tomorrow? In that case we should start making plans for the village today. I want to visit this site you've found and Knut's already promised to help us. Now, we'll need several longhouses, a blacksmith's, a drying hut, stables, a palisade, naturally—'

'Later.' Danr protested before she got carried away. 'I'm too tired to discuss anything sensibly. Right now, I'm going back to bed. Brandt may be able to survive with no sleep, but I can't.' He tugged on Sissa's hand. 'Come on.'

'Do you want to mate again?' She looked at him curiously. 'After this morning?'

'That wasn't what I was suggesting.' Danr stifled a smile as Hilda started coughing. 'But now that you mention it...'

'You *do* both look tired.' Joarr came to the rescue, his own eyes bright with amusement. 'You should probably *both* go back to bed.'

'Good idea.' Danr gave him a swift grin. 'If you'll excuse us, Stepmother?'

'*Are* we going to mate?' Sissa asked again as they made their way back through the village and into the hall.

'Yes!' He couldn't stop himself from laughing this time. 'Although you should probably stop calling it that or Hilda is going to have a fit. Yesterday I wouldn't have cared, but I've made a promise to look after her now.'

'Oh.' She looked perplexed. 'What should I call it instead?'

'Perhaps we need some kind of secret code.' He drew her into their private chamber and closed the door firmly behind them. 'Maybe...'

'Playing *tafl*?'

'Perfect.' He placed his hands on her hips, leaving not the tiniest sliver of air between them. 'In that case, when we get back to the forest we're going to play *tafl* every night. Repeatedly. At length. In every variation I can think of. When we're not actually playing *tafl*, that is.' He frowned. 'Actually, this could get confusing. Maybe we should call it—'

'You talk too much, Norseman.' She laid a finger against his mouth. 'You always did.'

'There's only one way to shut me up.'

'I know.' She replaced her finger with her lips. 'And I don't want to hear another word from you for at least an hour...'

Epilogue

Spring, ad 878

'Danr!' Sissa stood at the entrance to the cave, waving frantically as he emerged from the trees.

'What is it? What's happened?' He came running at once. 'I was helping Joarr with one of the roofs and it took longer than I intended. Has it started?'

'Yes!' She wrung her hands at the sound of a low howl from within. 'I don't know what to do!'

'She knows what to do, don't worry. Just be with her.' Danr glanced over to where Halvar was trotting up and down and whining. 'In the meantime, I'll stay with him.'

'Yes, good.' She pressed her forehead briefly against his and then hurried back inside the cave, crouching down on her haunches at a far enough distance for Tove to see, but not be disturbed by, her. The female wolf was turning around and writhing in circles, in obvious discomfort though the only sounds she made were occasional whimpers.

The passing minutes were interminable, drifting on into what felt like hours, but eventually there were four cubs, their small pink bodies all nestled against Tove's side.

'Four!' Sissa declared, going back outside, feeling drained but triumphant.

'Male or female?' Danr stood up from where he was sitting on a rock.

'Two of each, as far as I can tell. Their eyes are still closed, but they're all moving and they look healthy.'

'Two of each…' He ran a hand over his chin thoughtfully. 'Well, Erika and Bersa, obviously.'

'We're naming them?'

'Of course. Are you honestly telling me you haven't been thinking about names?' He lifted an eyebrow. 'One of the males could be Rurik. I'd love to see my brother's face when I tell him.'

'All right, and the other can be Frode.'

'Frode?'

'It was my father's name.'

'Then Frode it is. If you're certain?'

'I am. You're my new family, but I never want to forget my old one.'

'Erika, Bersa, Rurik and Frode.' Danr smiled lovingly. 'I feel like a proud father.'

She laughed and rolled her eyes. 'Don't tell Hilda or she'll start getting ideas. She already looks at my stomach every time she sees me.'

'Really?' He glanced downwards.

'Don't you start! I'm not sure how I feel about going through childbirth after watching that.'

'Ah, but you'd have me with you, holding your hand and talking the whole time.'

'Exactly! There's no hurry anyway.' She stretched her arms above her head and sighed. 'Much as I enjoy playing *tafl*, I'm happy with things as they are for a while longer.'

'About that...' He drew his brows together. 'Joarr said there was a message from Brandt this morning.'

'Oh!' She caught her breath. 'What's happened?'

'To be honest, it was more of a summons.'

'A summons?' She folded her arms determinedly. 'You're not going anywhere without me, Danr Sigurdsson.'

'I had a feeling you might say that.' He slid his arms around her waist, pulling their bodies together and gazing deep into her eyes. 'In that case, it looks like we're going to Maerr.'

* * * * *

If you enjoyed this story, be sure to read the first three books in the Sons of Sigurd miniseries

Stolen by the Viking
by Michelle Willingham

Falling for Her Viking Captive
by Harper St. George

Conveniently Wed to the Viking
by Michelle Styles

And don't miss the next story in the Sons of Sigurd miniseries, coming soon!

Tempted by Her Viking Enemy
by Terri Brisbin

Historical Note

The Isle of Skye is the second-largest of Scotland's islands, located off the north-west coast and home to some of the most striking geological formations in the world. It was known to the Vikings as Skíð—misty isle—or Skýey—cloudy isle—probably in reference to the weather that surrounds the famous Black and Red Cuillin mountain ranges that dominate the landscape.

According to the *Book of Kells*, the first known Viking raid on the island was in AD 794, with the first Norse settlers arriving in the late eight hundreds, when my story is set.

One problem I discovered while researching, however, is that historians are surprisingly vague about the ninth century on Skye. Although evidence such as carved stones and *brochs*—round towers—suggests that the early people were Pictish, it seems likely that by this period they had already adopted the Gaelic language and become part of the Dal Riada confederation, having more in common with Irish Gaels than Scots.

The old Irish romance *Scéla Cano meic Gartnáin*, for example, is based on rival families in Skye. For this reason, I've chosen to refer to the indigenous people as Gaels while focusing my story predominantly on the Norse population.

While Orkney remained the nominal centre of Viking power in Scotland, the 2011 discovery of a dockyard, complete with canal and stone quay, on the Rubh an Dunain peninsula suggests that Skye may have been a more important location than previously thought.

Whatever the reality, the island remained part of Viking territory for the next four hundred years, up until the Battle of Largs in 1263, which finally returned the island to the Kingdom of Scotland.

This book has been fun to write, as well as slightly intimidating, as it forms part of a series with Michelle Willingham, Harper St George, Michelle Styles and Terri Brisbin. We came up with the overall storyline together, although we developed our own books independently—the first time I've done this kind of collaboration.

I hope readers enjoy the series as much as we've enjoyed working together. A huge thank you and a hug to all of them!